BLOOD PASSION

BOOK IV
MALEVOLENCE

J.M. VALENTE

Cover by J.M. Valente

ReadersMagnet, LLC

Blood Passion: Book IV Malevolence
Copyright © 2020 by J.M. Valente

Published in the United States of America
ISBN Paperback: 978-1-951775-90-2
ISBN Hardback: 978-1-952896-56-9
ISBN eBook: 978-1-951775-91-9

All rights reserved. No part of this publication may be reproduced, stored in a retrieval system or transmitted in any way by any means, electronic, mechanical, photocopy, recording or otherwise without the prior permission of the author except as provided by USA copyright law.

The opinions expressed by the author are not necessarily those of ReadersMagnet, LLC.

ReadersMagnet, LLC
10620 Treena Street, Suite 230 | San Diego, California, 92131 USA
1.619.354.2643 | www.readersmagnet.com

Book design copyright © 2020 by ReadersMagnet, LLC. All rights reserved.
Cover design by Ericka Obando
Interior design by Manolito Bastasa

REVIEW

J. M. Valente's BLOOD PASSION~BOOK IV~Malevolence, is relevant to a heart pounding walk on a lonely, desolate stretch of road, on a dark, foreboding night, with only your imagination, fear and thoughts as your companions.

Once again, Valente cleverly cultivated Rachael Valli, bringing forth a human hybrid Vampire, who walks in both worlds.

Rachael, now herself a newly published Author, having assumed the guise of Mia Harkness, is thrown into a maelstrom of notoriety; appearing for numerous book signing engagements, proposing a fear of discovery, perchance aggravating her very demise.

J. M. Valente, ever the Artful Master of the Macabre, has cunningly crafted what is a riveting BLOOD PASSION Fourth Novel. Complete with an ending that will permeate to the very core of one's soul.'
'A Truly Magnificent Read'

—Jeannie Scott Flynn

ACKNOWLEDGMENTS

*Thanks once again,
to my Beta reader,*
Jeannie Scott Flynn,
*For keeping me inspired.
And a special thanks to*
Ken Dodge
*Of Castalian Springs, TN.
For his insight for the epilogue,
Once more to my*
Ginger Editing Program,
& Amazon Fire Tablets.

DEDICATION

To all my loyal Fans/Readers,
That sincerely love, and enjoy, my
Writings a.k.a. Storytelling

CONTENTS

Chapter One 1
Chapter Two 5
Chapter Three 10
Chapter Four 15
Chapter Five 20
Chapter Six 24
Chapter Seven 28
Chapter Eight 32
Chapter Nine 36
Chapter Ten 40
Chapter Eleven 44
Chapter Twelve 48
Chapter Thirteen 53
Chapter Fourteen 57
Chapter Fifteen 61
Chapter Sixteen 66
Chapter Seventeen 70
Chapter Eighteen 74
Chapter Nineteen 78
Chapter Twenty 82
Chapter Twenty-One 86
Chapter Twenty-Two 90
Chapter Twenty-Three 93
Chapter Twenty-Four 98

Chapter Twenty-Five 102
Chapter Twenty-Six 105
Chapter Twenty-Seven 108
Chapter Twenty-Eight 112
Chapter Twenty-Nine 116
Chapter Thirty 121
Chapter Thirty-One 124
Chapter Thirty-Two 129
Chapter Thirty-Three 133
Chapter Thirty-Four 137
Chapter Thirty-Five 141
Chapter Thirty-Six 145
Chapter Thirty-Seven 149
Chapter Thirty-Eight 154
Chapter Thirty-Nine 159
Chapter Forty 163
Epilogue 167

One 173
Two 177

CHAPTER ONE

RACHAEL VALLI NOW using the alias name Mia Harkness, sits, relaxed, gazing out from the window in her newly acquired second floor corner room at the, Riverside Bed and Breakfast, in the town of Sleepy Hollow, NY, simply watching the Hudson River sinuously roll by on the other side of the Road. Thinking,

'So this is to be my new digs for now, not bad, and the manager's name is Michael. He even resembles my real Father Michael Valli's Dad, Michael Sr., weird, but somewhat comforting in its own way. After Dinner, which I believe they said it is served in the Dining Room around six, and it gets darker, I'll go out to my car and bring in the rest of my bags that has my money in them. After that, I really should take the time to give it a good counting so I will know where I stand as far as my finances are concerned. So what do I wear for Dinner, really don't have much to choose from, actually need to go get some more clothes, like soon?'

She finds a skirt to wear with the blouse she already has on and feels that will do just fine, so she puts it on. Just as she sits to begin fixing herself up for Dinner, she then hears a commotion outside her window that overlooks the front of the building, she then brings out her Vampiric enhanced hearing ability so as to hear what is being said out there.

"Mike! Mike!" Young Ben yells excitedly, as he runs up the front stairs onto the porch where Michael is sitting, "Wait till I tell you what's headed our way!"

Michael stops him with,

"Benjamin my boy, sit down and catch your breath!"

"Yeah yeah, I will, but I just have ta tell you, it's so cool!"

"Okay, calm down, and tell me what's so cool that has you so excited?"

Ben sits and begins to breathe regularly as he starts to explain,

"You're you're not going ta believe it!"

"Ben please relax, just tell me what it is that has you all keyed up?"

"Yeah yeah, you're just not going to believe what I just saw and heard up on the main road at Pete's Garage and Gas Station. It's just so cool! You're not going to believe me!"

"Ben please, you're rambling, just tell me, already!"

"Yeah yeah, I will but…"

Mike agitatedly cuts him off,

"Ben, just tell me! I do have ta go in soon to help my Sister with getting tonight's Dinner Menu ready."

"Well, Mike, well, up on the main road at Pete's Garage!"

Mike edgily cuts him off again,

"So help me, Ben, if you don't get on with it."

"Okay, so there I am, just hanging out, enjoying a bottle of Soda, when this really cool, I mean a really boss Harley Davidson Motorcycle, pulls in for gas and directions, and you will never guess to where!"

Mike grabs Ben's arm and says demandingly,

"Young man, you're making me crazy, just tell me!"

"Here, Mike! Pete told me, that they're coming here, Mike! Coming here!"

"Yes, I'm expecting a new guest, besides the new one we already have!"

"Well, you just wait till you see this one!"

"Oh, yeah, okay, I just can't wait," Mike declares, humoring Ben, and continues

"But like I said Ben, I really need to get in now, to help with the preparations for tonight's Dinner Menu!"

Just as Mike starts to get up from his porch chair, he catches sight of an extraordinary looking Motorcycle, with a somewhat strangely clad Operator pull into the parking lot.

Ben excitedly proclaims,

"See see I told yah, I told yah! That's the Bike! Oh man, that's the Bike!"

"Yeah, yeah, Ben relax and just chill out, or you're going to bust a gut, it's just our new guest."

"Just, our new guest! Look at that; have you ever seen anything like that, just look at that excellent Harley Davidson Motorcycle? Sooo Bit-chin!"

"Okay, Ben now compose yourself, and let's greet our new guest cordially, and get'em checked in."

Ben standing awestruck, ever so slightly nods his head in agreement, letting out a faint panicky muddled mumble.

This Rider parks, and dismounts, shifts their clothing and lifts the tinted Helmet Windshield to take a look round, to get a better feel for their surroundings. Mike and Ben both stand somewhat motionless just staring in awe, of what they can see on the back of this person, as the Rider removes their Helmet places it on the seat of the Bike, shakes out their long dark hair, and puts on a Black Leather Low-Rise Cowboy Hat taken out from one of the Saddlebags.

What they curiously observe, in total amazement is a very mysterious looking character, adorned in Black Leather riding apparel with what looks like purple embossments of Angels' Wings on the back and sleeves of their Jacket. When this individual finally turns round and slowly begins to walk towards them, wearing Boots that are even more impressive; Black Leather of course, with what appears to be a Silver embossed Skull on the front of each of them, and also more extraordinary are the Boots' thick gleaming Silver heels that sound loudly with every step they take on the pavement of the parking lot.

When this mysterious person reaches the top step and then onto the porch with a rucksack in tow, and then steps closer to both Mike and Ben, they are both standing in complete wonder, of what they are witnessing, after all, this is one incredibly impressive vision of dread, and beauty wrapped up into one dynamic looking Woman. She then removes her Black Leather Cowboy Hat with a Silver Cross adorning one side of it, unzips her jacket, and greets them announcing, in what certainly is a mysterious, but rather melodious authoritative Southern accent,

"Howdy, gentlemen, I do indeed reckon, this is the Riverside Bed and Breakfast, of your lovely town of Sleepy Hollow, in this here grand state of New York?"

Mike quickly shakes off his dismayed status, and responds to her, as he motions to her to the side door, while Ben stands beside him, somewhat still frozen in place.

"Yes, yes it is Ms., welcome, would you please step into the Lobby, and we'll get you registered, straight away."

Mike then nudges Ben, back into awareness, while informing her,

"Then my young assistant here, Benjamin, will show you to your accommodations."

Ben abruptly comes out of his dazed state, with an ear-to-ear grin on his face, timidly stammering,

"Yes yes, plea plea please step, I... I mean enter!"

Mike quickly opens, and holds the door open for her, so she can walk inside, and over to the counter to check in. Mike swiftly makes his way round the counter, and hands her a pen. She takes it and signs her name in the register,

Angel Seraph.

CHAPTER TWO

Michael turns the Registration Log-Book around to be able to fill-in the room number, then turns round to grab the room key, before handing it to her, he looks at her full name in the Log-Book and takes notice of her first name, and states respectively,

"My goodness, Angel! That's quite the unique first name you have there, my Dear."

She responds nonchalantly,

"Yes, I suppose so. Is there a problem with my name?"

Ben, sitting behind her on the Lobby Bench, waiting nervously, he chimes in with,

"I like it. I… I love it!"

Angel turns to look down at him seated on the Bench, giving him a smile, she responds,

"Why, thank you, young Sir, I do appreciate that!"

She then turns back to Michael and asks somewhat firmly,

"Well, Sir, is there any problem?"

"No no, by no means, no my Dear! Here's your key. May I be so bold, as to ask; your eye color, are they… Purple?"

"Yes, they are Purple, just like Elizabeth Taylor's were."

"And Ms. Seraph, I must add, just as striking."

"Thank you, Sir. That's real sweet of yah."

"Ms. Seraph, there's really no need for you to call me Sir."

"Well, then, how shall I address you?"

"My name is Michael; you can call me Mike, everyone does."

As she begins to make her way to the staircase to the second floor, she turns her head, smiles and answers to him,

"Then Mike it shall be, and please, do call me, Angel."

"Will do," he responds back, with a smile and adds,

"Dinner should be ready about six."

"Sounds grand, see yawl then!"

Mike then addresses Ben still seated on the Lobby Bench,

"Ben… Ben… Benjamin!"

Ben still in a state of awe, having been spoken to by Angel, does not immediately respond.

Mike raises his voice a little,

"Ben… Benjamin… Earth to Benjamin!"

He finally comes to attendance and looks up at him. Mike than clears his throat, points to the Rucksack on the bench beside Ben, and then shifts his eyes toward the staircase.

Suddenly, in the archway leading from the Lobby to the Dining room a young girl appears, and addresses Mike,

"Uncle Mike, my Mom says she needs you in the Kitchen right away!"

"Yes yes, Cathy, tell her I'll be there, in a minute."

Ben bolts up to be standing in front of the Lobby bench, grabs the Rucksack, and starts for the stairs following directly behind Angel.

He has an eclectic thought as he follows her down the hallway,
Oh my God, She smells heavenly.

As they approach the door at the corner room of the opposite end of the Building down the hall from Mia's room. Ben maneuvers his way around to be in front of Angel, puts out his hand for the room key. She then places it in the palm of his hand.

At about the same time Mia has heard them in the hallway, so she, being curious, cracks her door open a bit to try to get a look at who's out there, seeing the front of Ben but only the back of the Woman, she thinks,

Well, that's Ben, but who's the Woman, I suppose I'll find out sooner or later.

She then softly closes her door, and goes back inside to continue getting herself prepared to go down for Dinner.

Ben unlocks and opens the door, stops to let her enter; she looks around and says,

"Yes, this 'ill do nicely."

Ben places her Rucksack on the bench at the foot of the bed and announces,

"We serve an awesome Dinner in the Dining Room about six; Mike's Sister Jeannie is an awesome chef!"

"Yes, Mike told me about Dinner being served about six," She makes known to him and continues with a request, "Ben, I left my Bike Helmet outside on the seat of my Bike, would yah be a dear, and go get it for me?"

Without hesitation he answers excitedly,

"Not a prob, I'll be right back with it!"

With that said, he walks backward to the door and then races out down the hallway and out to the Parking Lot to find her Helmet just where she said it would be, but before going back to her room he circles her Black and Purple Custom made Harley Davidson Motorcycle to get a closer look at it. When he comes around the other side he sees something that gives him pause, what he sees is a powerful looking weapon hung on the left side of the front fork of the Bike, he touches it gently with one finger and thinks,

Wow, this is one bad-arse looking weapon, some kind of shotgun or hand held canon, looks to be automatic too.

He then grabs it a little tighter, but can't move it. He says softly aloud,

"It's in some way locked to the fork of the Bike."

Then he thinks,

Good thing, I didn't set off any alarm when I did that.

Letting go of it, he walks to the back to look at the two large Purple Saddlebags, which also have locks on them. He then notices that they are both decorated with what are like large Silver Crosses. He reflects in awe,

This sure is one Bit-chin Motorcycle, for a fab looking Lady, can't help but wonder what she does and who she is, no sense in asking, she probably wouldn't say, leastwise not to me, best to mind my business.

With that thought, he heads back inside to give her the Helmet. Finished with this chore and getting for himself a grateful tip from her. He goes to sit down at his station, which is the Lobby Bench.

Mike comes into the Lobby wiping his hands on a Kitchen towel, seeing Ben, he asks of him,

"So Ben, is our new guest settled in?"

"Yeah, Mike, you just have 'ta see her Harley, it's unbelievable and…"

Mike cuts him off with,

"Benjamin my boy, I realize it's a Custom job. Really pretty, right?"

"Yeah, but…"

Mike again cuts him off, sternly saying,

"Ben, you're needed in the Dining Room to help do set ups, we have a larger than usual number of Dinner guests this evening. So please, hop to it!"

With his head lowered and uttering under his breath a grumble, he slowly makes his way into the Dining Room.

Angel gets out of her leathers, freshens up, changes into something more relaxed and comfortable, and heads down for Dinner.

The first thing Ben set his eyes on is, as she descends the stairs, are her Black Leather Cowboy Boots adorned with Purple Wings embossed into them. He thinks,

She's one awesome surprise after another!

He continues to watch her descent; he couldn't take his eyes off her if he wanted to. What appears next is striking also; she's wearing tight glossy black leggings with what looks to be a purple silk tank top. As she steps onto the floor at the foot of the staircase, the light from behind her makes her earrings glitter which gives off a shine in her long dark hair, giving the effect of her having a halo around the back of her head. Ben has another silent observation,

Oh man, her earrings look like Purple wings! And is that a halo I see, or just a trick of the light, that is sooo Bit-chin!

She addresses him and asks,

"Hey Ben, do I need to be seated for Dinner?"

"Yeah, our hostess Cathy, will be here to help you in a moment."

"Okay, I can wait. Should I ring the Desk Bell?"

"No need, she'll be here shortly."

This is Ben's honest effort to have more time, to be in her presence

CHAPTER THREE

ANGEL LEANS HER back up against the Check-in Counter with her elbows posed back beside her for support, as she waits to be seated by Hostess Cathy for Dinner. With Ben seated on his Lobby Bench looking up at her, he states and asks,

"I happen to notice your accent. If I may be so bold in asking where are you from."

"I get that question a lot, especially up here in these parts."

"There, see, like that!"

"Yeah, I know, I've spent quite a bit of time south of the Mason Dixon Line."

"So, down south, I thought so. Where down south?"

"Well, I'd have ta say, mostly Baton Rouge, Louisiana? You know where that is, Ben?"

Trying to sound somewhat knowledgeable about U.S. Geography he answers,

"Well, I know where Louisiana is, but the city of Baton Rouge, not really too sure."

"Well, It's the Capital City, North West of New Orleans and just south of the Mississippi Border. Does that help?"

"Yeah, a little, thanks!"

Mike enters the Lobby from the Dining room and inquires,

"Angel, my Dear lady, something I can do for you?"

"Just waiting to be seated for Dinner, is all."

"I'm sorry, we're really busy tonight, let me just see if our Hostess Cathy, has a table ready for you, yet."
"Please Mike; I don't want to be any bother."
"Bother? It's no Bother! You're our guest here; it's no problem at all. Be right back."

Before Angel can say another word, Mike shows up with Cathy, and she addresses Angel,
"So sorry for keeping you waiting, Ms. Seraph, I have a table ready for you now, please do follow me,"
As they start to leave, Mike interjects with,
"Cathy, make sure she gets a free appetizer!"
Angel stops, turns slightly and exclaims softly,
"Oh, Mike, you don't…"
He cuts her off,
"Please, it's my pleasure. Enjoy!"

With Angel now in the Dining Room headed to her table, Ben stands up to quietly address Mike,
"Mike, she is from down south, some city in Louisiana, she told me so!"
"You couldn't have figured that out for yourself by her accent, Ben?"
"Yeah, Mike, I guess, but I wasn't sure."
"Ben, go into the Kitchen, and see if they need you to help out!"
"Wow, we really are super busy, tonight!"
Ben asserts, as he stretches his neck to peer into the Dining room. Mike harshly reiterates.
"Yes, we are Ben, Kitchen, go, now!"
Ben grumpily replies,
"Yeah yeah, I'm going, I'm going, Jeesh."

Mike goes behind the counter to check on a few things, and refill the Printer with paper as he bends down to get some paper, to put in the Printer, the Desk Bell sounds. When he comes up, he is greeted by Mia.

"Good evening Mike, can I be seated for Dinner now?"

"Good evening Mia, just let me see, give me a moment."

With that said, he goes into the Dining room.

Mike returns with Cathy. Cathy addresses Mia, now seated on the Lobby Bench,

"Hello, Ms. Harkness, sorry to say, but we are pretty full up right now, it's rather a small Dining Room, I can offer you a seat at a table now, if you don't mind sharing. Would that be alright with you?"

"I believe that would depend on, who with!"

"One of our recent female guests is eating alone; I don't think she'll mind sharing with you."

"Cathy, please go, and see if she would mind."

"Already did, she said she wouldn't mind at all."

"Okay then, lead the way!"

"Good, right this way, please!"

Mia follows Cathy the short distance to the table that Angel is occupying, and makes the introduction.

"Excuse me Ms. Seraph; this is Ms. Harkness your Dining partner for this evening."

Angel looks up and announces,

"Cathy, please, it's Angel."

Mia also announces to Cathy,

"And Cathy, please, it's Mia!"

Mia pulls out the chair on the opposite side of the table and says,

"Angel is it? Thanks for sharing your table with me."

"Yup, it is, and you're entirely welcome, Mia."

Cathy, then hands Mia a menu, declaring,

"Here you go, Ms. Hark… sorry Mia, we do have a limited choice, but all are wonderful, if you happen to have any special Dietary requirements, just let your wait person know, and please enjoy your Dinner!"

"Thank you, Cathy, I will."

Cathy leaves them.

After a short silence.

Angel speaks first,
"So Mia, I reckon we're two ladies, who are travelin' on our own?"
"Oh no, I'll be staying a while, I intend on finishing my Novel, or at least close to it. Right here in Sleepy Hollow, where it's so delightfully peaceful, and quiet."
"So, you're an Author!"
"Not yet, just a writer for now, this will be my first book, so not an Author until I'm published. Then I'll be one!"
"So that's how, it works."
"Yes, that's how!"
"And you Angel, if I may be so bold, what do you do?"
"Well, that's a mite hard to say, let's just say I take care of special things for the U.S. Marshals Department."
"Wow! A real U.S. Marshal!"
"Not a real Marshal, so ta speak, just a special Agent."
"Still, pretty cool to be having Dinner with you! Are you on a special assignment, right now?"
"No, in-between assignments, fixin' on leaving tomorrow, headed for the New York City Office, to be gettin' my next assignment."
"If I tell you any more, I'd have'ta kill yah!"
With that, Mia looks down, and softly giggles!

Their conversation is aptly interrupted by the Waitress.
"Excuse Me Ladies, but have you two made your decision on what you'd like for Dinner tonight?"
"Yes, I have," Angel answers, looks to Mia and continues,
"You, Mia?"
"Yes, I believe so."
The Waitress takes their orders and then motions to leave saying,
"Okay then, I'll be back with your drinks, and that appetizer, to get you started."

Simultaneously, they respond,
"Thank you. Ah?"
The Waitress hesitates, responding,
"It's Sara, and you're welcome."
She replies, then hurries off.

Another short silence.

Mia looks at Angel and questions,
"Angel?"
"Yeah, it's an old… ah, Family name."
"Your accent?"
"Oh, so you noticed that, did yah?"
"Somewhere down south, I'd say."
"You'd say, right."
"Let me hazard a guess: Georgia, Alabama, Mississippi, ah, no, wait I have it, Louisiana?"
"It's Louisiana, yup, Baton Rouge! Went through all this with Ben earlier."
"Okay, so then, I'll just leave it there."

After enjoying their lovely home cooked Dinners, they leave the Dining Room, and go their separate ways, wishing to one another, 'Good Night.'
On her walk back to her room, Mia reflects,
Wo, for a microsecond there, I thought I might have been her assignment. So glad I'm not.

CHAPTER FOUR

Angel Arrives In the Lobby at about ten in the morning, makes her way, with her Bike Helmet and Rucksack, to the Registration Counter, looking round, not seeing anyone about, she rings the bell. Within seconds Michael shows up, wiping his hands on a Kitchen towel, finishes wiping, puts it down on the shelf behind the counter, turns to attend her, in a jovial manner,

"Good morning, Angel, my Dear. Sleep well?"

"Yup I did, it's very quiet up here in these parts."

"That's why we like it, so much! What may I do for you, this fine morning?"

"I'll be Checkin' out, this here fine mornin'."

"Yes, of course, can we offer you something to eat first; we do have some freshly baked Muffins this morning, and we serve the best brewed Coffee around and we also have Tea, of course, or are you in a big rush to be on your way? We wouldn't want to keep you, from your business."

"Well, I reckon, I could manage a few minutes for a quick bite. A cup of your good Coffee sounds just grand, please!"

Michael smiles as he moves to the archway, and gestures for her to enter the Dining Room saying,

"Good, here give me your things and let me put them down behind the counter and come right in and have a seat, and I'll get you that Coffee. And one of our delicious Muffins, perhaps? We do have Corn, Blueberry, or Peach this morning!"

"I would fancy a Peach, thank yah!"
"Be right back!"
"I'll be, right here!"

Michael returns within minutes, with her breakfast order places it down in front of her, then seats himself in the other chair at the table, and inquires,

"So my Dear, you may not want to tell me, and that's okay, but may I ask, just where are you headed, and for what?"

"Well, Mike, I'm on my way to New York City on business, for my profession and just exactly what that is, I'd rather not say. I hope you understan', it's of a clandestine nature"

"Oh, yes, of course, I didn't mean to pry, so sorry, but I was just curious, that's all."

"That's just fine. By the way, where's my little 'Fan Boy' this mornin'?"

"I believe you're referring to Benjamin?"

"Yes'um, sure am."

"He usually comes in around noontime."

"Is he your boy?"

"No, he's an old friend of mine's Grandson, just lives the next street over, I started putting him to work around here in the summers, and he just kept coming around, to see if we could use him, so we, me and my Sister, decided to put him on the books. He's really a good boy, and a great help around here too, especially when we get busy, like we are right now!"

"That sure is real nice of you, Mike."

"Yeah, thanks. How do you like that Muffin?"

"Mmmm, liken' it just fine, remindin' me of home. And the Coffee is truly grand!"

"Well, we do try to please. Will we be seeing you back here any time soon?"

"I'd reckon so, if I'm ever up here in these parts again, it's been real nice stayin' here, with yawl!"

"Well, it's been very nice having you stay with us. You'd certainly be welcome to come back anytime; I'm sure young Ben wouldn't mind, at all, seeing you again, and that Bike of yours!"

Angel finishes her meal, and heads out to the Lobby with Mike right behind her, to settle up her bill. With that done, he walks her out carrying her things for her, hands them to her and watches as she secures her Rucksack to the seat, mounts and starts the Bike, then backs up to be able to pull out of the lot, she brings the Bike over to the stairs and stops, opens the Windshield of her Helmet and declares loudly to Mike, who is standing at the top of the Parking Lot steps.

"Mike, you be sure now, to be tellin' young Ben I said; goodbye and thanks!"

"Have no doubt about it, Angel, I will for sure, you be safe now!"

With that, she smiles, closes her Helmet Windshield, pulls up to the street opening, and with a roar of the engine; she gets underway south, down the road.

Mike turns in place, as he waves goodbye, even though she probably doesn't see him do it, as he watches her pass by the front of the Bed and Breakfast.

Mia sits in the easy chair in her room sipping her wine, which she had brought in late last night, along with the rest of her luggage; she hears the roar of a Motorcycle engine pass by her shaded front window and without looking outside she just supposes its Angel leaving for New York City.

After taking the count of the money, she brought with her, to find that she has more than enough to last her for quite a while.

She then takes out her Laptop Computer, places it on the desk, plugs it in, opens it, and turns it on, so to get back once more, to the writing of her Manuscript. Now seated at the desk, with her wine glass set beside the Laptop, she places her fingers on the keys and begins;

Mia opens her eyes to see Marcus getting dressed, so she inquires of him,

'Marcus, where are you going this morning?'

'Mia, sorry to wake you, I need to see Nantinus to receive my expenditure of funds for our journey Northwest.'

'Northwest? Why are we going, Northwest?'

'Because my Dearest, the rural town we will be going to is in that direction.'

'And what town is that, my Love?'

'Woodstock, Vermont!'

'Woodstock! You mean that town, where that big historic Rock Concert was held, back in the Nineteen Sixties?'

'Yup, I think that was the one! I shant be long,'

He then continues to inform her as he's closing the door,

'You can make ready to go, while I'm gone.'

She answers him with a simple, affectionate, 'Yes, my Love.'

Marcus makes his way down the hall, of Victus' large Mansion on the hill overlooking the Mystic Bay, only to observe Lucus walking towards him. He braces himself for a possible confrontation, they lock eyes, and both of them slow the pace toward each other, like two Gunfighters of the Old West at High Noon on the Main Street of Tombstone, as the space between them slowly diminishes, both of them are having feelings of expectation, which could likely lead to a physical altercation. As Lucus comes closer a wry smile appears across his lips, and he says as they embrace,

'Marcus, ma Boy! It is good to see that you had the good sense, to come in on your own, I was growing a little weary of the chase.'

Marcus replies snidely with,

'Yeah, I could tell, when you attempted the kidnapping of Mia to lure me to come to you!'

Parting from their embrace, Lucus now with his hands on Marcus' shoulders, lets out a robust laugh, and Marcus follows suit, but not so robust. They then part by stepping aside from one another, and without

• •

another word, continue in their respective directions. A few steps taken, at the same instant, they both look back at each other, to exchange a relevant wave.

CHAPTER FIVE

BENJAMIN COMES RUNNING up the front steps of the Bed and Breakfast, excitedly shouting,

"Mike! Mike!"

Mike quickly comes out the front door, to greet Ben irately,

"Ben my Boy, calm down, please!"

"But, Mike it sounded like... I mean I definitely heard a Motorcycle going down the road, was it her, oh please, oh please Mike, tell me that it wasn't her and that she's not left yet! I... I set my alarm early enough to wake me, just so, not to miss her leaving, Mike, please tell me that wasn't her Bike I heard going down the road."

Mike moves to Ben's side and puts his arm over his shoulders in the effort to comfort him, and walks him through the Dining room, then into the Lobby, requesting,

"Ben, please, calm yourself my Boy, I'm sorry, but that was her leaving, that you heard."

Distraught Ben lollops onto the Lobby bench, lets out a heavy sigh, and hangs his head and says,

"Oh Man, Mike, she's gone, I missed her, what a major Bummer! I really wanted to help her get on her way, and to see her, just one more time."

Ben hangs his head, Mike attempts to console him comfortingly saying,

"Ben listen to me, my Boy, Ben, please look at me!"

Reluctantly, Ben slowly lifts his head to look up at Mike, as Mike continues to say,

"Ben, she did tell me to be sure to let you know that she was very appreciative of all your help. Also, she told me that if she's ever back this way again, she'll definitely stop in, and maybe even stay here for awhile."

Ben slowly stands up, with his head lowered; he proceeds through the Lobby to the side door muttering,

"Yeah yeah, that's just great, but how long will that be…."

His words fade as he exits the door.

Michael goes about his business thinking,

Poor kid, looks like he's having his first broken heart.

Up in her room Mia heard some of the commotion, not really getting enough of it, to make any sense out of it, she goes back to her writing,

Mia and Marcus in the early evening begin their journey as they travel West on Route Ninety Five through Connecticut, until they get to the junction of Route Ninety One where they will turn North, up through Massachusetts and eventually into Vermont. About half way up through Massachusetts, Mia requests that they stop somewhere, that she might be able to freshen up and get a little something to eat. Marcus makes a sound in agreement and noticing a sign for Northampton, turns off the Highway and heads in the direction of the Downtown Area. He reaches over and gently takes her hand in his, saying,

'There should be someplace you can get what you want in this town. We should be there real soon, okay?'

She gives his hand a lovingly squeeze and replies,

'Thank you, you're so sweet!'

He points ahead and informs her saying,

'See, the lights of the Downtown Area are right there, just up ahead! I myself could do with a glass of Wine.'

Mia takes out her Cellphone to look up restaurants in the area, the first one that comes up on her screen is at the Historical Hotel Northampton, she tells him about it and he immediately agrees to take her there saying,
 'Now that sounds really nice.'
She just looks at him to give him a pleasant loving smile.

 Suddenly a gentle knock sounds on Mia's door. She pushes back from the desk and proclaims loudly,
"Coming!"
And thinks,
Now who can this be?
As she approaches the door, she hears a familiar voice saying,
"Ah, Ms. Harkness, it's me, Benjamin."
As she opens her door saying and asking,
"Good evening, Ben. Whatever do you want?"
"Well, Ms. Harkness, the Kitchen is closing in about thirty minutes, I was wondering if you desire anything before they do!"
"Well, Ben, that's so sweet of you, I guess I could go for some Tomato Soup. If they have any?"
"They sure do, had some myself tonight, it's real good. Would you like a cup or a bowl?"
"I think a cup would suffice, thank you."
"Something to drink with that, Ms....?"
Mia cuts him off,
"Ben, please, it's Mia!"
"Oh yeah, sorry, Mia!"
"That's all right Ben, but from now on it's Mia. Okay?"
"Oh yes, of course... Mia!"
"I have my own beverage, so I'm good with that."
"Cool, I'll be back in a flash, with your Soup!"
"Please Ben, don't hurry."
"Okay, Mia."
 With Ben gone, she slowly closes the door, turns round and walks to the window overlooking the Hudson River, after seeing its

reflection in the water, she looks up at a beautiful full Moon, lets out a long sigh and softly murmurs,
 "A Bella Luna night."

CHAPTER SIX

MIA SITS IN the easy chair by the window, just looking out into the night, sipping her Wine, when she unexpectedly sees reflected in the window her eyes have turned to red, and practically at the same time the red mist in her vision appears, and then goes away about as fast as it came. She puts her glass down, and lays her head on the back of the chair, closes her eyes and retorts softly uttering,

"Damn you Malevolence and my Blood Passion curse!"

And then an optimistic thought enters into her mind,

It's been a while, I was hoping my condition might have gone away. Just some wishful thinking I would have to guess, because how could a condition that I was born with, ever go away on its own?....

Her thoughts fade and her eyes close, as she unknowingly and ever so slightly dozes off.

Suddenly there's a knocking, actually more like a scratching, at the door of her room. A strange but slightly familiar ominous voice using her real name, calls out from the other side of the door.

"Rachael, I have your Soup!"

This unusual voice makes her respond comatosely, like a Zombie,

"Yes, Ben, just a minute, I'm, I'm coming."

She slowly and dutifully rises from the chair, walks to the door, throws it open wide, but it's not young Ben that's standing there, it's a horrifying vision of the noticeably decayed body of Marlena, with her mouth open wide, wider than any normal human mouth could ever open, showing unusually long rather corroded Blood stained fangs. This horrific image jolts her to awareness, and she abruptly wakes to find herself back by the window lollopped in the easy chair. Righting herself and breathing a little uneasy, she leans forward, bows her head, puts her hands over her face and thinks,

Just a really dreadful nightmare, that appalling thing could never ever be for real, I hung her body up on a broken tree limb some time ago, and the morning sunlight dried her up to nothing more than a pile of dust that the wind blew away, she's gone, long gone! Is that how I will go? Will I, at some point, not be able to go out in daylight at all, not even on an overcast day? Also will I ultimately become a creature of the night, like my real Father and Marlena; who was Mother's best friend, as well as my Godmother?

Her numerous inquiries are interrupted by another knock sounding on her door, she hesitates at first to rise, so as to, compose herself, then rises slowly, not sure if it's just another dream. But she must answer it, to find out, no matter what or who it might be. She steadily gets herself to the door, and gently but firmly puts her hand on the doorknob, asking,

"Ben, is that you?"

He ingenuously answers her,

"Yup, Mia, it's me, I've got yah Soup!"

She lets out a slightly relieved sigh, opens the door slowly this time, to see thankfully that it really is, young Benjamin with her cup of Soup.

"Oh, Ben, it is you!"

"Yeah, why, where you maybe, expecting someone else?"

"No, no, not at all, I just dozed off a little and wasn't sure if, the idea of you bringing me the soup, was just a pleasant Dream I may have had."

"It's no Dream, and it's really good Soup, too. And after you have it you will feel like you just might be in Heaven, it's that good really, so where'd you like me to put it, for you!"

Mia, has a sudden thought,

Heaven, that's someplace I'll presumably never see.

"It's that good, Ben?" She points, instructing him,
"Over there on the desk will be fine."
"Yup, it's that good!"
He proclaims as he places the cup of soup on the desk with a few packages of crackers. As Mia gets her purse to get him the money for the Soup and a tip for his kindness. He gratefully accepts it, with her gratitude, and backs his way out of her room, stops at the threshold to ask her,
"Would there be anything else I can get, or do for you?"
"O, Ben, you've done enough already... ah wait a tic, can you tell me where a girl may get herself a drink around here on a lovely night, such as this?"
"Around here, well let me see, my Granddad and my Dad go occasionally to the Tavern up on the main road, to watch the Sports Games and stuff with their friends, it's called 'The Horseman'. It's sort of across the Street from Pete's garage and Gas Station. You know where that is, right?"
She proclaims, and questions,
"Yes, I know where Pete's station is. The Horseman?"
"Yeah, 'The Horseman' I guess it's named that, because of the..."
"Yeah Ben, I'm familiar with that old fable, Ichabod Crane and all that."
Ben just smiles, as Mia reiterates,
"Well, thanks again for the room service and for the info about the nightlife around here."
"No prob, anytime, good night, and you keep your Head!"
She replies in kind, as he turns and walks away. Before closing her door, she leans out to scrutinize the hallway, for anything odd looking, then straightens up to close her door and make it secure.
She tops up her Wine glass, and sits at the desk to enjoy some of the Soup, thinking,
Keep your Head! Silly Kid. Although, this Horseman Tavern just might have some possibilities, it's such a nice night too, I'll just have to take a stroll up there later, and check it out. This Tomato soup, wow! It's

all Ben said it is. Mmmm, will be even better with a splash of my Wine added to it!

Mia finishes the cup of delicious Tomato soup, rinses out the cup in the bathroom sink, and looks through her over-night bag to see what she has left to wear to this Tavern. To her pleasant surprise she finds her cream colored Satin Blouse that will go just perfect with her short black silk pleated skirt, and feels she'll look just fine for this part of her new world.

It's now a little after eight in the evening and she begins to make herself ready to go, she'll be walking, so only a comfortable pair of shoes will do. Luckily she has her pair of cream colored Prada flats with her.

She stands in front of the full length mirror holding the garments up in front of her and thinks,

This should do just fine, stylish but not overstated.

She lays them on the bed, disrobes to take herself a shower. With her Shower finished she fixes her hair, and makeup, adorns herself with a pretty black lacy bra, because with her blouse slightly unbuttoned, it will show a glimpse of it, just enough to provide that come-on guise, and a sexy attitude!

All made up, and dressed, she once again stands at the full length mirror, unbuttons the top two buttons of her blouse, feels its not enough, so she unbuttons one more and says snidely,

"Yeah, this should do it," and continues with a wry smile on her ruby red lips,

"Come into my parlour, said the Spider to the Fly! Yeah, let's just see, what kind of Flies they have around here."

She then grabs her gold clutch bag and makes her way down the hall to the side staircase, then out the side door, avoiding the front Desk. She then makes her way to Riverside Drive, leisurely follows along it, as the River flows on the other side of the road, just enjoying the beautiful Night, and the comfortable Weather, until she comes to the first street that will take her up to the main road, noting to herself, just what a beautiful night, it really is,

It truly is a Bella Luna Night.

CHAPTER SEVEN

MIA WALKS NONCHALANTLY along, making her way up to the Main Road and eventually to this Tavern called, 'The Horseman', just enjoying for herself the beautiful Night, so much so, that she stops to sit on a small Bench close to the Street, in the front yard of a House, very close to where this Street meets the Main Road, as she leans back and looks up at the Full Moon, to her it seemed suddenly to turn red, but only with her because, it was her vision possessing the Ruby Mist. This being, the second time in one night that her vision appeared to have the Red Mist, definitely tells her that she's in need of a Blood Passion feeding, rather soon, more than likely, this very Night.

She swiftly rises from the Bench and walks a little faster now, to make it to the Main Road, in which the Tavern is located. Now, seeing in the distance a small wooden sign, lit up by a spotlight just above it, she walks in that direction, just before she gets to it, she takes notice of a small Women's Clothing Shop that is closed for the Night, looking in the Shop Window, she spots several things that take her fancy, and she makes a mental note to return when it is open for Business. In this Window noticing her reflection, she makes sure she is looking her best, with a show of approval she winks and thinks,

Looking good, Girl!

Mia enters the Tavern and takes a seat at a place of the Bar that is not too busy, on the other end of the Bar, there is an elevated large screen Television, mounted high enough on the wall, so that the several Men that are grouped can watch what looks to be the end of a Sports Event of some type. The Bartender, who is also somewhat engaged in the watching of this Sports Event, has heard the Tavern Door open, and close, turns round to notice her and dutifully approaches, asking,

"Good evening, Miss, what's your Poison?"

"My Poison as you put it, is a glass of Red Wine, thank you!"

"Coming right up!"

He accommodates her with her order, and goes back to watching the Television.

As she sips her Wine, she spies a rather handsome mature looking Man, which seems to be off on his own not very much engaged in watching this Sports Event. They look in each others direction, their eyes meet, he smiles, so she winks, and then with his drink in hand, he moves off his stool to the empty one next to hers' at the Bar, then as he sits, he playfully addresses her,

"Hi, come here often?"

"Now, when was the last time I heard that one? Ah, let me see…"

Before she can answer her own rhetorical Question. He cuts in with,

"I'm so sorry, that was dumb; please permit me, to start over. Good evening, my name is James Val…"

Quickly placing her finger gently on his lips, she declares,

"Please last names are not necessary, nice to meet you James, I'm Mia."

"Mia, lovely name, you may call me, Jim."

"Jim, is that what they call you around here?"

"Not really, I'm not from around here, just passing through on Business."

"Business trip, uh?"

"Yeah, this is my First one around here. Hey, your glass looks like it could use a top up. May I be so bold?"

She answers him,

"Yes, you may, thank you, that would be very nice,"
And she thinks,
He seems perfect for what I need tonight, just what the Doctor ordered, as they say.

James replies, as he signals the Bartender for a round.

"Yeah, I generally think of myself as a nice Guy, if I do say so myself! So, Mia, do you live round here?"

"No, just on a sort of Sabbatical, really need some peace and quiet to be able to finish my Novel."

"Oh, a Writer, that's cool! May I ask what your Novel is about?"

"Well, you may ask, but you may not care for the subject matter."

"Please, enlighten me."

"Well, it's mostly a Romance Story; I really don't think you'd be interested in it."

"Come on, just because I'm a Man, you don't think I'd like a Romantic Story!"

"Well, most Men don't really go for those types of Stories."

"I'd say that's a little opinionated of you. Wouldn't you admit?"

She smiles and answers,

"I wouldn't admit, to anything."

With that, they both laugh.

"I tell you what; this place is going to be closing soon. How's bout, I show you just how Romantic, this 'Man' can be?"

"And just how are you going to accomplish that, James?"

"Well, it's quite simple really, it being such a very nice Night; I suggest, you and I take a Romantic Moon Light walk along the Hudson River. What do ya say to that?"

She answers,

"I'd say, that sounds really nice, and sort of Romantic, I do believe I'll take you up on your offer."

With her acceptance of his invitation, she has a thought,

And I also believe, I just may have found my Fly.

Laughing again, they rise off their respective bar stools, James pays the Bar Tab, and together they leave the 'Horseman Tavern'.

As they walk into the Night air, James takes in a deep breath, and claims,

"Ah, it is a lovely Night, and just look at those Stars and the Moon, looks so large and close. Appears close enough that you could just reach out, and touch it."

"This, James, this is what my Grandfather would refer to, as a 'Bella Luna Night'!

James, comments inquisitively,

"A 'Bella Luna Night'?"

She answers, and explains,

"Yes, a Night in which the Moon appears to be incredibly large and rather beautiful in the Sky. Like you said, almost as if you could reach out, and touch it."

"Well, then, I wholeheartedly agree, with this Grandfather of yours!"

As they continue to stroll along, Mia has yet, another thought,

Oh yeah, I've definitely found my Fly.

CHAPTER EIGHT

MIA AND JAMES, now strolling along the wooded bank of the Hudson River, the light from the beautiful full Moon filters through the trees. She walks slightly ahead of him so that he will not notice, when she brings out her night vision which makes her Eyes turn red, for her to be able to see like it is Daylight.

They come abruptly to a small, well lit clearing, where she immediately retracts her night vision powers, and turns around to face him with her hazel Eyes. He keeps walking slowly towards her, forcing her to walk backward until her back is up against one of the trees, on the far side of this clearing, he puts his hands gently on her shoulders and bends in to attempt to kiss her, she turns her face away to avoid his physical advances, and with her hands on his chest she applies a small amount of resistance but still keeping him close, and questioningly she says,

"So, by the way on a curious whim, what is your full name?"

He straightens up to answer her,

"I thought you didn't want to know it. Didn't you say that last names weren't necessary?"

"Yeah, well, I changed my mind, it's a Woman's prerogative to do that, you know."

"Yeah, I guess so."

He remarks.

"So, what is it? Well, what are you afraid of?" And with a wry smile on her lips, she continues, "Come on, I'm not a Monster, I don't bite, much. Come on, give it up!"

"Okay, ya, it's… it's Valente, James Valente, but like I said before, everyone that knows me, calls me, Jim."

"May I call you, Jim?"

"Sure, if you'd like."

"I would."

He bends in to her again, in the attempt to nuzzle her neck. Without him noticing she kicks a small broken branch with her right foot into the river, and frightfully questions,

"What was that?"

He abruptly brings his head up, and looks to her right, which makes him turn his head to look over his left shoulder, that gives Mia clear access to his neck, and in this same instant her Eyes turn red and her Fangs extend, she quickly puts her arms around him to hold him fast, as she opens her mouth wide to swiftly sink her long Blood sucking Fangs into his skin at his neck.

Before he can even somewhat conceive what is happening, she has taken enough of his Blood to make him go weak and helpless in her arms, and now without any resistance from him, she can finish her much needed life sustaining Blood Passion feeding.

When she has taken just about all of his Blood, and he let out his last breath with his heart stopped beating, she lets go of this body, where it falls to the ground. She bends down to remove any things identifying of him, she comes up with his Wallet and uses the light of the Moon to see that he really is this James Valente person, he claimed to be. She then throws the wallet and anything else that could be connected to who he is, into the River, and then easily pushes his body down the bank and into the water with her foot, with the strong current quickly carrying everything away. She leans back up against a tree to revel in her much needed feeding, which has replenished her strength once again, and then her Eyes, Teeth and finger Nails return to normal. She takes out her compact mirror from her clutch bag to check for any Blood that may be around her mouth and wipes it away with a makeup remover Wetnap. Shifts her clothing and composes herself to make her way back to the Riverside Bed and Breakfast, enters in the same door, she left from, and straight up to her room, changes into her sleep wear and robe, not feeling at all tired, decides to do some more writing of her Manuscript. She opens her laptop and while it's coming up, she pours herself a glass of Wine, sets it down beside the computer, then sits to get back to her writing once again.

Mia and Marcus now back on the road to their destination. Mia, after enjoying what she can see of the lovely scenery out the car window turns to Marcus to ask of him,
 'Marcus, my Love, where will we live?'
 'Well, my sweet, the Cabal has a safe house known as the 'Woodstock House' up in the state of Vermont; where we can stay as long as we like to plan our next move."
 'Sounds nice. But who is there or takes care of this place?'
 'Janus, is the Caretaker, he is rather old, but not as old as Quintus, I believe they are related in some way, thou.'
 'Like you and your Brother, Victus?'
 'No, not Brothers, I don't think. But something close to it, I would surmise,' He informs her, and continues,
 'Up there, this faction of the Cabal mainly survive on the Wildlife's Blood, and then sells the Meat in a small private Butchery at the back of the house, where the locals come to buy it for themselves, they are given a very reasonable price. It's worked that way for quite some time now.'
 'Sounds as civilized as it could be, I would have to say.'
 'And you'd say right, my Love!'
 They arrive at this 'Woodstock House' and are welcomed warmly by Janus and his staff. Marcus is well received; they are taken to the third floor Master Suite. Entering Mia proclaims with approval,
 'Wow; now this is very charming and comforting! Just like a real Vermont Bed and Breakfast would be!'
 'I'm so glad you like it, Mia!'
 'I do, I really do! It's truly lovely, here!'

'Marcus, I will need to, as soon as possible, do some clothes shopping, thou. You rushed me out of my place so fast; I really didn't have much time to gather a lot of my stuff. Is there a nearby place I can go to?'

'Yes, by all means, Mia, one of the Human Staff will accompany you, just as soon as you'd like.'

She questions, his statement,

'Human Staff?'

'Yes, my Love, there are Non-Vampyres working here, as well as Vampyres, and it is perfectly safe for them to do so! The arrangement I explained to you, keeps them safe. They are essential for the Daytime operations of this place. Let me assure you, my Love, they are and have been perfectly safe working here for years, just as you will be safe here as well, after all, we need them, and I need you, Sweetheart!"

'Wow! Humans and Vampyres working together, side by side, who woulda' guessed. Not me!'

Marcus just looks at her and lovingly smiles, and replies,

'Yes, there is a whole other world, you would have never known about if we had not met!'

Now, she returns the Loving smile, finishing his statement,

'And fell in Love!'

Together, they look at each other and in agreement proclaim,

'Yes, absolutely!'

CHAPTER NINE

U.S. Marshal Agent Adams knocks on the door of Captain Stern's Office. From inside the office he hears,

"Come in!"

The door opens and Adams sticks his head in and announces,

"Captain Stern, excuse me, Sir, Special Agent Ms. Angel Seraph has arrived."

"Good, send her right in."

As Angel enters, the Captain requests of her, as he's hanging up his Desk phone,

"Please, Special Agent Seraph, have a seat. And please pray tell. How did the assignment in Michigan go?"

"Well, Sir turns out to be one of them there, False Alarms."

"We're really sorry about that, Special Agent Seraph."

"Please, Sir, everyone at the Washington DC, Main Headquarters Office calls me Angel, so I reckon you could also."

"Thanks, I will. Want to tell me about this False Alarm? I'd really like to hear about it."

"Well, Sir, there just ain't much for the tellin', but iffin' you really want to know, then I guess I should tell yawl, what precisely went down."

The Captain adjusts himself in his Desk Chair, and leans back saying,

"Good, I'm all ears, shoot!"

Angel gestures with her hand in the shape of a Gun, pointing at the Captain, and in her mind, she thinks,

Bang!

And then she begins,

"This here Man, weren't no actual Werewolf at all, although he truly believed that he is or was, so sad, and just between us and the wall, Captain, like some folks down South would say, a true 'Cuckoo Bird', so I right quick, apprehended him, and I'd like ta add, off the record, 'Nut Bag', without too much of a fuss, I turns him over to the State Authorities and they take him away lickety-split, for a Mental Evaluation at their local Hospital, and really that was all there was to it."

"Sorry, about that, Special Agent… I mean, Angel."

"Heck, that's all right, Captain. The best part about it was, I was able to stay at this really nice place for the night in the town of Sleepy Hollow up there, on your Hudson River, as a little rest from my drive to come here. So, Sir, what yawl has for me next?"

The Captain casually sits up in his Desk Chair, clears his throat and pulls open the middle drawer of his desk, and removes a red Folder, puts it down in front of him, opens it, gives it a quick glance, just making sure that it's the right one, then hands it across his Desk to her saying,

"Here, have a look for yourself."

She leans forward to take it from him, puts it down on her end, of his Desk, opens it, and begins to read, suddenly she stops, irately closes it, looks up at him, declaring strongly,

"A Witch! Really, Captain, a Witch! This Woman in Salem, Massachusetts, honestly believes that she's a real, pointed Hat wearin', Broomstick ridin', honest to goodness, Witch. Good Lord, Captain!"

"Yeah, well, I don't see any goodness to it, and I don't, in fact know, about the pointed Hat, or the Broomstick riding things, but yes, according to the report file, she actually believes, that she is a, bonafide Witch."

"So what's the problem, what do ya want me ta do about this, Salem, Massachusetts Witch Woman, Captain? Really!"

"Well, that's a little hard for me to say."

She agitatedly responds,

"A little hard for you ta say! Whatcha mean, by a little hard for you ta say? All ya have'ta do is open your mouth, and let the words come out!"

"What I meant is, I'm not sure how you would, or should approach this one."

"So, you don't have anyone else for this one! Were ya even fixin to send someone else there, besides me?"

"Well… no! You were the first of our Agents that came to mind for this type of assignment, after all, we don't have anyone better than you for these cases, and it does fall into the Category of the Supernatural. That is, what you do best! Right?"

With a smirk, and a slight undertone grumble, Angel takes the folder off his desk, from where she had laid it down, leans back in her chair, and opens it once again, to read a little more about it, and then quickly puts it down in her lap, lets out a deep sigh, and declares,

"Okay now, seein' as you ain't got anyone else for this, right?"

The Captain just nods his head in agreement, as she continues,

"And I do appreciate the agencies' confidence in me, so I reckon I'd have'ta be the one to go take care of this. And Captain, there are these types of Women in the South, but down there they're known as, Voodoo Queens!"

"Good, then you have some idea of what you're up against, so you take the File with you, study it in your Hotel room tonight. You are staying at the Plaza, right?"

She happily replies,

"Yup!"

And he adds,

"Nothing but the best for you! So, when you're ready to go there, you just let me know."

Angel leisurely stands, with the Folder in hand, and leaves Captain Stern's Office. As she slowly walks through the waiting room, she pauses a moment, removes her Leather Cowboy Hat, jerks her head aside to shift her hair, putting her Hat back on, she resumes her exit.

Attentively watching her, from the Reception Desk, U.S. Marshal Agent Adams hears her agitated soft murmur as she, slowly closing the Door behind her, looking down at the Folder in her hand.

"Good Lord, a Witch, what in Heavens name, could they have for me next!"

CHAPTER TEN

IN HER SUITE at the Plaza Hotel, Angel studies what there is of, any particulars of this Salem Witch Case File. Making notes in her mind, and in her rather full Case Note Book, of this Witch's description and her exact location in the City of Salem, Massachusetts. With that done, she then opens her Laptop to research Witches in general, looking to find out just what these New England Witches may, or may not be capable of. Most of what she finds to be generally Folklore, and Legend, even some Fairytale references. She laughs slightly, when she reads a little about 'Hansel and Gretel', because in the Case File, it is reported that this Witch in Salem, has been giving out or trying to give out Candy to Children passing her house, almost every day.

With a slight smile on her face, she slumps back in her chair, and decides that she will definitely handle this Case, if for nothing else, then for the protection of Children against a potential threat that could do them some harm, so she will leave New York City right after Lunchtime, also will contact Captain Stern at the U.S. Marshal's Office of her leaving, and then again when she arrives at where she will be staying, her base of operations, so to speak. On the internet, she has acquired a Room Reservation at the Historic Hawthorne Inn of Salem.

She sighs, and remarks aloud,

"It sure is a crazy Job, but someone's gotta' do it! And I reckon it should be me, bein' what I really am, an all."

She straightens up in her chair, and gently but firmly slaps her hands on the arms of the chair. As she stands up to pour herself another cup of Coffee, from the room service Breakfast tray, that was brought to her room earlier. She proclaims, simply thinking aloud,

"Yup, sure as shootin', that is after all, why I made the decision to come down here. Yeah… it sure is!"

She then walks over and stands at the Window sipping her Coffee, just gazing out at the tremendous Skyline of this Grand Old City of New York, her translucent reflection seams, just for an ephemeral instant, to show a large pair of white wings spread wide open behind her, somehow attached to her back. She blinks and they vanish from her reflection. She reaches her hand back over her shoulder to feel nothing unusual, so she shakes it off as just a trick of the light, and then proceeds to get herself cleaned up, and dressed, then after that gather together her effects, for her four hour journey north, wanting to be ready to go right after she gets herself some Lunch.

While enjoying her pleasant Lunch at The Palm Court Restaurant in the Hotel, she receives a call. Her cellphone display shows, Gabrielle, and immediately she answers it,

"Hey, Sis, Whatcha' doin'?"

A female voice agitatedly answers her,

"Angel, where are you?"

"Here in 'The Big Apple', New York City, and fixin' to be headin' even further north soon, for a new assignment, long story, really can't talk right now, sorry, talk soon! Okay?"

"Yeah, okay, but you best make it soon!"

"I will, promise, love ya Sis, bye!"

Gabrielle replies in kind, and they both hang up.

Finished now with her Lunch, she goes up to her room, to finish gathering up her things and call the Front Desk to send up a Bellhop for them, also have them notify the Hotel Parking Garage to have her Harley ready to go within the hour. As she's collecting her Toiletries from the Bathroom, she hears what sounds like tapping on the sitting room window, with avid curiosity, she goes to the window to see what could be producing this noise, after all she is up on the sixth floor; at first she sees nothing, so she moves a little closer, she begins to see white tail feathers. She moves right up to the glass and looks down on the ledge, spies a large white Mourning Dove, appearing to be in a rather nervous state, walking along the ledge back and forth. It must have flown up here, and almost slammed into the window, but safely landed on the ledge. She begins to imagine how the wings appeared in her reflected ghostly image in the window. It must have been flying right at her, as she was looking down at the People in the Street, not really seeing its body, only catching a glimpse of its wings, as she brought her head up, which made it look like the wings she saw, were on her back. She steps back from the window, and says,

"Poor thin', I hope it gets itself down," she stops, and thinks for a moment, lets out a soft giggle, and continues, "What am I thinkin' it's a Bird, it surely can fly its way down,"

At the door a knocking sounds, she calls out,
"Yes, who is it?"
A young Boy answers her,
"Bellhop!"
"It's open, come on in."
A young man enters saying,
"Hello, Ms., if you please, show me what you want taken down to the Lobby, and I'll gladly accommodate you."
"Yup, it's the things on the bed, just take 'em out and I'll follow you to the Lobby to collect em', and be settlin' my Bill, thanks… umm."
"It's Billy, Ms."
"Good, okay, you do that, whilst' I say, so long to my new Friend just a sittin' on the window' ledge."
Billy begins to disbelievingly repeat her words,
"New Friend, on the…?"
She quickly turns round to him, cutting him off with,

"Yeah, a lovely Bird landed there and I just wanta' say, so long, that's iffin' it's still out there."

Billy gathers up the few items that she has on the bed, puts them on his cart in the Hallway, looks at her through the open door of the room, with a smile on his face that's holding back his laughter, and then quickly makes a start for the Elevators.

Angel, now in the Hallway just a few steps behind him, sadly announces,

"It's gone, my new Friend left without even sayin', so long!"

Humorously Billy replies,

"Yeah, for some unknown reason, they do that a lot around here!"

They both burst into laughter at this, just as the Elevator Doors slide open. On the ride down in the Elevator, to the Lobby, young Billy has some thoughts,

She's a little strange, but the beautiful ones usually are, Man, she's a real looker, as the guys in the Neighborhood would say, she's the Bomb! And smells Heavenly too, mmm. Wish I was a little older.

CHAPTER ELEVEN

AFTER DEALING WITH everything at the Hotel Front Desk, she makes her way, followed by Billy, with his Hotel Luggage Cart to the Garage, to acquire her Harley, lode it up then head for Salem, Massachusetts. After putting her trappings away, then checking that all the Locks and that her Shotgun is secure, she approaches Billy to give him a handsome tip for all his help, then settles her parking bill, plus a tip for the Garage attendant. The attendant takes her payment, thanks her for the tip, and compliments her on her awesome looking, customized Harley Davidson Motorcycle, she thanks him. Then, he asks her,

"So, my Darlin', where you headed, now?"

"Well, I'm fixin' to head north, up to the City of Salem, Massachusetts, yup, got me some important business up there, to take care a'!"

"That's about a four hour, plus ride for you, if you're travelling through Connecticut, be sure to have yourself a nice Meal in the town of Mystic, at the Mystic Pizza Restaurant, it's on Main Street. You do like Pizza, don't you?

"Yup, sure do, thank ya for the tip!"

With a roar of the Bike engine, she takes off.

They watch as she turns the corner and is gone. Billy looks at the attendant, and articulates,

"That is one awesome looking Lady, and that Motorcycle, oh yeah, that's' a Hell of a Combination!"

"Yes, but more like a Heavenly Combo, I'd say, and that Southern Accent of hers' is to die for!"

Billy playfully replies, as he begins to push the empty Cart to the Elevators.

"Yup, you sure, got that right!"

With that they both let out a small chuckle.

Suddenly there comes a soft knocking on Mia's Door, She stops what she is doing, and slowly walks up to the Door and inquires gingerly,

"Who is it?"

The familiar voice of Benjamin replies,

"It's me Ms. Harkness, Ben!"

With very little hesitation, she swings open the Door, asking him,

"What up, Ben, what is it? And by the way, didn't I tell you to address me by my first name of, Mia!"

Yeah, you did, but...!"

"No buts Ben, everybody annoyingly, way to often has a big but! So, like I said. What up, my 'Man'?"

"Just wondering if you're hungry, is all. There's some more of that really good Tomato Soup available this afternoon, Jeannie made another large Kettle of it for the Lunch and Dinner Menu!"

"That sounds just, excellent. Would you bring me a Cup?"

"Only a Cup? You know how good it is, and it really goes fast!"

"Okay okay, a Bowl then, you'd make a really great salesman!"

"For Jeannie's cooking, it's an easy sell here in Sleepy Hollow, all right, Mia, back in a flash!"

"Please, take your time, Ben, there's no need for you to rush, really!"

As she begins to slowly close the Door. He requests,

"Anything you need to drink?"

"No, still have some of my bottle of Wine left."

"Okay, good!"

Then he vanishes down the Staircase.

She now closes and makes the Door secure, then slowly goes back to the Desk to continue, what she was doing when, and before Ben knocked, and that is staring at her Manuscript on her Laptop screen. She finally gives in and admits in her thoughts,

Writer's Block! That's what I have, it's Writer's Block! A Blood Passion feeding usually gives me plenty of inspiration, but not this time. Writer's Block, damn!

She Questions,

What was it I heard about, what Writer's Block is?

She hesitates for a moment, trying to remember,

Oh yeah, it's when your imaginary Friends stop talking to you.

She quietly giggles, and continues to just sit, staring at the screen, with her elbows on the Desk with her chin, and cheeks in her Hands, pouting. Then, out of the blue, it dawns on her, as she rereads the part in her Fiction Novel, where her imaginary Female counterpart desires to go Clothes shopping. She now continues in her thoughts,

So, that's what I'll do. Right after I have some Soup, I'll drive up to that little Women's Clothing Shop up on the Main Road, that I spotted last night, on my way to that charming little Tavern, and get myself a few nice things that I saw in the Display Window, just maybe some new things will do the trick, and spark my imagination back to life. Could be a win win for me; a few new things and also revive my creativity for my Fiction Story.

Angel notices the Statue of a Witch in the Center of the City of Salem and stops to read the brass Plaque on the ground in front of it, she learns that it's a Tribute to the lovely Actress 'Elizabeth Montgomery' who played a Witch named 'Samantha', on the long running Television show titled 'Bewitched' from the Nineteen Sixties to the early Nineteen Seventies, she thinks,

Oh, that's just grand, these folk here, give notoriety and respect to a Witch, and I have'ta attempt bringin' one to Justice, just cant' wait to see how this' ill' pan out. I just might be getting myself, run outa' town on a rail.

After checking her notes, to refresh herself on the Hotels' location, she makes her way to this Historic Hawthorne Inn, to check in, get settled and make the call to Captain Stern. She also has a loving thought about the only Man in her private life; Victor, who resides down in Atlanta, Georgia, that she hasn't had much contact with, in way to long. A quick thought comes to her mind,

The Man ain't called me in awhile, eitha', I'm sure hopin' he's still round, to be in my life, that is. I'd best be given' him a call right soon. I'll do it after I talk with the Captain. Busy, busy, so many Crazies, so little Time.

Once settled into her Room, she makes the call to U.S. Marshal Captain Stern. He gives her the instructions, to make contact with, Salem Police Chief Jeffries, to get the latest update on things, but is too late for that now, so she'll have to wait until morning. This now gives her the opportunity she wanted, to make contact with Victor, but first she calls the Front Desk, to politely requests that they send up a Pot of Coffee to her Room from the 'Tavern On The Green' Hotel Restaurant. While she's waiting for the Room Service delivery, she makes herself comfortable by changing into her lovely White Silk Lounging apparel, and not long after she does that, the Room Service arrives with her Coffee, along with a complementary Apple Pop Over and a Cinnamon Scone. She graciously accepts the delivery, bestowing on this person a polite gratuity.

CHAPTER TWELVE

After Angel Has her Coffee, and little Snack, she pours a second Cup, and then she picks up her Cellphone and places her call to Victor,

Surprisingly a Woman's voice answers,

"Hello, Victor Vincent's', line!"

"Hey? Where's Victor, and who the Hel…?"

"Just a moment, please, here he is," This Woman cuts her off handing Victor the phone.

Not knowing who it might be that's calling, this very attractive, tall, dark, and handsome Man, addresses the caller,

"Hello, this is Mr. Victor Vincent!"

"Nice to hear that you ain't too busy doin' what ever', to take my Phone call!"

With pleasurable recognition he reacts,

"Angel!"

"Well, looky there, you remember me!"

"Angel, don't be silly, course I remember the Woman, I'm in Love with!"

"Vic, I simply must ask. Just where in the heck, are yah?"

"You remember that little town just outside of Cairo, Egypt, where we first met. Don't yah?"

"Course I do! Much ta hard to be forgettin' that place!"

"Well, Sugar, I'm back here on business, handlin' the shippin' of some Egyptian Artifacts, which are on loan to the Smithsonian in Washington DC, that was Elsa, answerin' my Phone for me, she's the Curator of the Egyptian History Museum in Cairo; she's here over seein' the Transport Operations, I was under one of the larger statues checkin' on the packagin' of it, just makin' sure it's secure enough for travel. She was merely holdin' my Phone for me, I told her to answer it, iffin' it rang, just because I'm expectin' an important call from the Smithsonian, they will want an update, on how things are goin' here, and I just thought it might be them calling, is all."

"Is that all, she's a holdin, for ya?"

He answers her, scoldingly,

"Angel! Please!"

She timidly, but defensively replies,

"Well! It's been awhile!"

"Yah for both of us, my Love. And yeah, that is all, she was, or ever will be holdin' for me, so please be nice!"

"Okay, good, I'm sorry, so when should yawl be back in the States?"

"Hey, yah know how this goes; I'll fly back to DC with the shipment, and then supervise the set up of the display, then iffin' I want to, head for home, I've some time off coming, ta me. And you? Are ya on one of your secret assignments again?"

"Yup, but I'm spectin' this one to be quick, I should be in DC, by the end a' next week."

"Good, sounds ta me like we should be in DC at about the same time."

She replies, in an innocent manner,

"And just what do you, specially mean by that, my dear, Mr. Vincent, Sir?"

"Angel, don't play coy, you're just not that good at it! I'll just say, we could get us a room in DC at one of your favourite Hotels, before I head back to Atlanta, and you go on to your next thing."

"Vic, sweetie, now that do sound a mite suggestive, ya do know me, so well."

She quickly adds a thought,

He really doesn't know me at all, and I like it that way, deep down, I think he does too.

"Okay then Angel, I'll see ya then, be well, be safe, you have my Love."

"And you be too, and you have mine, my dear Mr. Victor Vincent, Sir."

With that, they both end the call.

A thought comes into Angels' mind,

Okay Gabrielle's turn.

While dialing, she pours herself another Cup of Coffee, It rings about six times, but just before it goes to voice mail, and she's about to hang up, Gabrielle answers, sounding rather breathless, hastily expelling,

"Not a good time, talk later!"

Then abruptly ends the call, Angel hangs up thinking,

I reckon I know what she's a doin', but with who, or is it whom? Never can seem ta get those straight. But want the heck it don't matter', just as long as she's havin' herself a good time!

Mia leisurely browses this little Sleepy Hollow Woman's Clothing Shop and has found a few things she likes, and a few of the things she needs. She brings them to the check out counter. The young blond woman there, inquires,

"I do declare! Ya found a few things that ya like!"

"Yes, a few I like and a few I need. Actually, this is a nice little Shop you have here."

"Well, ya, but it ain't mine it's my Aunt Anna Beth's. Hence, the large lett'as A.B., on the Shop's sign on the front Door, and display Windows."

"You will excuse me Miss, but do I denote a bit of a Southern Accent, in your voice?"

"Yah sure do Ms., my Aunt Anna Beth met a man from round here on a Cruise Ship on the Gulf, awhile back, so she came up here to marry him, my uncle Peter, and not too long after that, she opens this here little Shop."

"Is that Peter, like in Pete's Garage and Gas Station?"

"Yup, one in the same, he's gotta' a few more of em' round these here parts!"

"If I may be so bold. When did you, come up here, and from where?"

"Well, I came up here not to long ago to be helpin' her out, she been feelin' rather poorly these days. I'm from a little town in Mississippi, that I'm just supposin' you ain't ever heard of."

"You will please, enlighten me?"

"Okay, yeah, it's… Eden, Eden Mississippi!"

"Yeah, well I certainly know the State and its major Cities, but you were right, I've not heard of that one!"

"Well, like a told ya, it's a rather small place, but we like it just fine."

"Yes, you did tell me, and I'm sure you do like it, but what you haven't told me is your name. I'm Mia. And you are?"

She executes a petite curtsy, and announces,

"It's my real pleasure to meet you, Ms. Mia, I'm Rose! Real happy to make your acquaintance, I'm sure!"

"Same goes for me, Rose."

As she rings up Mia's choices, their conversation continues,

"So Rose, do you like it living up here in the North?"

"Well, it's okay, I'm a guessen', but, there's a few things, I do miss."

"Exactly what, for instance?"

"Like, Warmer Winters, for one."

"Anything else?"

"Yup, the food, but we cooks mostly Southern Style at my Aunties place, wherein' I live with 'em, so it ain't so bad, I'd rightly so, be admittin."

With Mia's shopping spree now completed, as she, with her large bag, begins to leave the Shop, Rose genially states,

"Thanks yawl Ms. Mia, for shoppin' here with us, we really do appreciate your business, and yawl have yourself a truly nice night, and yawl come on back and see us, real soon!"

Mia responds in kind, as she slowly closes the Shop door,

"You're welcome, I just might be back soon, and you have yourself a good night too! Rose, from Eden, Mississippi!"

CHAPTER THIRTEEN

MIA WALKS IN the Riverside Bed and Breakfast Lobby with her large bag from the A.B. Ladies Shop, seeing Michael behind his counter, just going about his routine business, that he does just about every day, she briskly walks up to the counter, stops and excitedly addresses him,

"Michael!"

He suddenly stops what he is doing, looks up at her with a stern but pleasant expression on his face, she immediately knows why, so she rewinds by taking a few steps backward and approaches him again greeting him this time with,

"Hello, Mike!"

Now, he answers her with a jovial smile,

"Better! Yes, my dear, what might I do for you?"

"Did you know about the Lovely Ladies Shop up on the main road?"

"Of course I did, that's my Cousin Pete's Wife's place, all the Ladies around this area shop there! But I heard that his Wife, Anna Beth, isn't fairing too well lately, that's sad, she's such a Delightful Southern Woman, I believe, they are known as Dixie Belles. Anyway, she came up here about ten years ago just to marry him, that lucky old curmudgeon! I wouldn't mind, having myself a Charming Southern Belle in my Life!"

Mia interrupts him,

"Maybe you should, book yourself on one of those Gulf Cruises that your cousin Pete went on, and possibly meet one, of your own. And, yeah, the very nice Young Woman at the Shop told me most of that."

Mike replies,

"Oh yeah, like I have the time and money for that. And, yes, I did hear that the shop is still open, regardless of Anna Beth's condition. And by the way, who is this very nice Young Woman tending the Shop for her?"

"So you were listening to me, her name is Rose, and she's really very nice! She even put a small New Customer Twenty Percent off Discount Card in my bag, for my next visit. And I did see a few things I just might go back for."

"Mia, I can talk, and listen at the same time. Did you say Rose? I do believe that's Anna Beth's niece from…"

And they simultaneously announce, profoundly,

"Eden, Mississippi!"

"So, Mike, how do you know all this stuff? Town Cryer or something?"

"No silly, My Sister Jeannie, you know, my Business Partner, and our awesome Chef, shops there from time to time when she has the time, and God knows, even with me and all the other help we have around here, she rarely gets a lot of time for female pleasures. Mia, why didn't you just get all the things you wanted today? While you were there?"

"Now, Mike, really, where's the fun in that. Gives me a good reason to go back there again, soon!"

"Oh yeah, how stupid of me! I didn't think, sorry."

"Mike, why wasn't I told about that place, before?"

"Mia, there's a Brochure," He points out, as he puts his finger on a small pile of them on the counter, and continues, "Right here on my counter, for that Shop, and a few more Brochures for some other places round here, too. Have yourself a look, and take the ones you want to your room with you. We used to put them in the rooms, but most of our guests would just throw them away, so we now keep them here, in the Lobby, so they can take the ones that interest them."

"And, Mike, getting back to you, and your Sister, I've been meaning to ask you, what is your Family name?"

"Well, my Dear, I suppose, to satisfy your youthful curiosity, I'll have to tell you, our Family name is, a rather old, and well recognized surname round here, it's… Van Garrett!"

"Oh my God! Isn't that one of the names connected with that Spooky Tale of the 'Headless Horseman', Ichabod Crane Story that was published sometime in the early Eighteen Hundreds, I believe?"

"I suppose, but, that was quite a long time ago, and never proven to be a true account, I believe Washington Irving, just used the local Family's names in his short fiction story, just to give it a slight ring of truth. Which I assure you, my Dear; it is not a true story, not a shred of truth to it, at all… Mia!"

"Yeah, but Mike, for a little Fictional Tale, it sure made this area quite Famous! I just wish that, what I'm writing could have somewhat of the same impact!"

"So, Mia, that reminds me, I've been meaning to ask you. How's that story, you are writing coming along?"

"I never told you I was doing that. How on Earth did you know that I'm writing a Novel?"

"Young Ben mentioned that you always say that you need to get back to your writing, when you are shooing him out of your room. He's not being a pest. Is he?"

"No no, he's been more than helpful to me, in more ways than he could ever imagine, he's a great kid!"

"Well, if he ever gets to be a pain or a nuisance, you just let me know. Okay?"

"Yes, Mike, I would, but I really don't believe he could or would ever be either of those! And speaking of Ben. Where is he today?"

"Some after School activities I would surmise, nevertheless, you let me know right away if he becomes a bother!"

"Yes, but…"

"No Buts, you know what they say about Buts. Right?"

"Yeah, I know that one!"

"All righty then, I have to go see if Jeannie needs me in the Kitchen for anything."

"Yeah, Mike, we can talk later, have a good night!"

Mike just gives her a little wave, smiles and leaves the Lobby.

Mia puts a few of the Brochures, that spark her interest in her bag, so with her shopping bag in tow, she happily makes her way up the stairs, back to her room, to get another look at the new things that she purchased, and have a closer look at these Brochures, of the other places in the area, just might come in handy, for her other things she could need, or would want to do.

CHAPTER FOURTEEN

ANGEL PULLS HER customized Harley Davidson Motorcycle up to the front of the Salem Police Station, dismounts, removes her helmet, secures the Bike, and begins to make her way into the building. She had made phone contact with Chief Jeffries earlier and they agreed upon a mid morning meeting, as she enters the building, the two Officers at the Front Desk take notice of her, one of them calls quietly to the other, who is busy filing some papers, requesting,

"Paul, come here quick, and get a load of this! You, really have to see this for yourself, to believe it!"

"Yeah, Frank, what is it?"

As he points to Angel, now making her way gradually, closer to them, Officer Frank softly states,

"Just look at that, will ya!"

Officer Paul admiringly responds,

"Woe! Now I've seen everything!"

Angel reaches the Desk, and genially affirms, in her charming Southern way,

"Mornin' Gentlemen, I am Special Agent, U.S. Marshal Angel Seraph here ta see your Police Chief, Jeffries, I do have a' appointment with em' this mornin', so iffin' ya would be so kind, I'd gratefully appreciate it for yawl would notify em' that I've arrived."

Officer Frank hastily picks up the phone, and makes contact with the Chief, tells him that his morning appointment is here, he listens for a moment, then says,

"Yes Sir," he then quickly hangs up, looks at Angel, informing her,

"He'll see you now, Ms. Seraph, I mean… Agent Seraph… I mean, I, oh, yeah, you can… please go right in!"

She shoots him a questioning look, insinuating. Where do I go? He leans out a bit over the counter, and points directing her, asserting,

"Oh, yeah, his office is right down the Hall, third door on your left."

As she begins to walk away, she proclaims,

"Thank ya kindly, Officers."

Officer Frank leans back in, sits down and states,

"Wow! Have you ever?"

"Chill out Man, she's just a Woman."

"You call that, just a Woman!"

As Angel enters the Chief's Office, he stands to greet her,

"Good morning, Agent Seraph, please have a seat!"

"Yes, Sir, thank yah. If yah please, can we get right to it, I've gone over the Report Case File. Is there any updates you can add that may not be in it?"

"Well, I've contacted our very own Salem Resident Witch about these complaints; she requested of this Department, that we let her handle it."

"Cuse me, Chief, but with all due respect, Sir. Your City has a Resident Witch?"

"Yes, she has been with us since the Nineteen Seventies, she usually monitors and handles all the Wiccan related incidents in our fair, City of Salem, Massachusetts."

"Sir, I'm up on the entire long past Witch History of your fair, City of Salem, and do believe I understand the need for someone like that. Are you spectin' this Resident Witch of yours to handle this case?"

"Well, see, there's the rub, she told me she'd handle it and I do believe her, but she has advised my Department to issue an immediate Cease and Desist order at once. This Woman in question is quite old and most likely a bit Senile; and we don't really believe she means the good Children of Salem, any real harm."

Angel counteracts somewhat irately,

"But, Sir, if I might be so bold, your Residents are, as we say down south, 'up in arms', and they be wanten' something done about this Woman, right quick! I mean, Sir, she's referin' to these children, by the names 'Hansel and Gretel', and I reckon yawl know how that little Story goes."

Chief Jeffries answers her, slightly heated,

"Excuse me, Agent Seraph, but something is being done about it, that is precisely why you are here, and I'm fully aware, of what she's calling these children. It's duly noted, in the Report Case File!"

With that, Angel stands, makes her way to the Office door to leave, she suddenly hesitates, looks back at him and sharply declares,

"Okay then, Sir, it seems we are on the same page, so how soon will a 'C and D' order be ready?"

"Most likely by, later today."

"Okay then, contact me on my Cellphone which yawl have in my credential papers, in front of yah right there on your Desk, just as soon as it is, and I'll come back for it, thank yah!"

"There really will be no need for you to be coming back here, to the Police Station."

With her hand still on his Office door knob, she shoots him a puzzled expression, as she begins to pose the question,

"And just how…?"

He immediately cuts her off,

"Please, Agent Seraph, settle down, and hear me out, I will have a Female Officer call you and meet you at the Dwelling of this 'Person of Interest', she will have the order with her, and you can both issue it to this…," He stops to refer to the Report Case File in front of him, "This, this, Ms. Wanda Norman, and then I'll notify our Resident Witch to take over from there."

"Okay then, I'll be a waitin' ta here from her?"

The Chief reiterates,

"This shouldn't take too long, so once you accompany her to carry out this task, and your part of the assignment is finished here, you'll be free to be on your way."

Now with this meeting seemingly concluded, Angel quits his Office, hesitates in the Hall, takes in a deep calming breath, and then proceeds to make her way out of the Building. However, she first stops at the Front Desk, to thank the Officers there, for their assistants,

"Thank yah, Officers for all yah help, yawl be having ya selves a grand ol' Day now, ya hear!"

Officer Frank responds,

"You're very welcome Ms., you have yourself a great Day also, and please do come back anytime!"

Outside, in front of the station, seated now on her Bike, Angel checks her watch to see that it's almost noon, and she finds herself feeling a bit peckish, therefore, she believes some lunch, would be in order right about now. So, she heads back to her, Hotel to have her lunch there in their 'Tavern On The Green' Restaurant.

While riding, she has some thoughts,

My goodness, this City actually has a Resident Witch, so glad I'm not dealing with her. So far this looks to be another of those False Alarms, again, but remember Angel, never, ever to underestimate a potential adversary. It ain't over till it's over! Although I'm yearning for an assignment with some real meat to it, truly ain't had one in some time, still the money and perks are just grand. Also, I'm a mite anxious to see and be with my Victor, again!

With that last pleasant thought, a considerable smile comes to her lips, she pulls into the Parking Lot of the Hotel, where she Parks, removes her Helmet, dismounts and secures the Bike. Now making her way to the Entrance Door, just thinking about what she'd like to have for her Lunch.

CHAPTER FIFTEEN

MIA FINISHES CHECKING out all the things she has bought at the A.B. Ladies Shop, folds, some and hangs the rest in the closet, then pours herself a glass of Wine, observing that the bottle is looking rather low, She slightly frowns in remembering that she only has three bottles left of this excellent special Wine, from what she took with her when she left the Cliff House in Mystic, Connecticut. She sits down at the desk, placing the Wine glass on the left side of the Laptop, opens her Computer, to once again get back to the writing of her Manuscript, places her fingers on the keys, ruminates for just a moment, bends her neck from left to right, then lets out a deep breath, and begins,

Mia sets down her shopping bags, in the Hallway just outside her room. Then softly knocks at the door. Accompanied by Lora, her Human shopping companion, she doesn't just want to go right in, just incase Marcus is in a state of undress. They both wait a moment for an answer, but hear no immediate reply, Mia takes out her room key, gestures to Lora to wait in the Hallway, then unlocks it and slowly opens the door, tenderly inquiring,

'Marcus are you here? Marcus? Marcus its Mia, I'm back from my shopping with Lora!' She then turns up the volume a little, 'Marcus are you here? Marcus?'

Marcus attentively appears from the Bathroom in his Robe, moves over to the dresser, swiftly taking something from the top of it, and places it into his Robe pocket, then greets her saying,

'Mia I'm sorry, I couldn't hear you come in, I was a little busy blow drying my hair in the Bathroom.'

'That's fine my love, just wanted to let you know that we're back, with all my shopping and tell you that Lora, was tons of help to me, she really knows her way around here.'

Marcus shoots her a curious look, questioning,

'Lora? Where is...?'

'Oh, She's still out in the Hall, Lora please, you may come on in now!'

Lora shyly enters the room, with the rest of the shopping bags, places them down, and graciously greets Marcus,

'Good afternoon, Mr. Marcus, Sir.'

'Lora, I don't believe I've had the pleasure.'

'Well, Sir, if you please, I just started a few months ago, and I do work mainly in the Kitchen; I'd really like to be a Cook someday, I took my Mom's place, when she found a fab job for herself at an upscale Restaurant in Montpelier!'

'And, pray tell, who is your Mother? Perhaps I know her.'

'Well, Sir, my Mom is...'

He instantly cuts her off,

'Lora, please, that's enough with the, Sir, you will please only address me by my first name, of Marcus!'

'But Janus told us to call you...!'

Marcus adamantly instructs her,

'Lora, my dear, regardless of what Janus says, you will please, refer to me as Marcus. I really do abhor this Mr. and Sir stuff!'

'Yes, Mr.... I mean Sir... I mean... Marcus!'

Mia turns to Lora, smiles and affirms,

'See, I told you, he's really very nice!'

'So, it looks to me like you two Ladies had yourselves a really nice time this day.'

Mia replies,

'Yes, my love, we really did, Lora and I had a wonderful time shopping at the lovely Shops, right here in Woodstock, and we even took the time to stop at a little place, and have an afternoon Tea break!'

Marcus interjects,

'And a little Girl Talk, I'd have to fathom a guess.'

Mia and Lora glance at each other, with a fanciful smile, as Marcus continues,

'So, young lady, just who is this Mother of yours?'

'Yes... my Mom, her name is Cathy.'

Marcus thinks for a moment, then informs her,

'No... sorry, doesn't sound familiar. Any others in your family, that work or have worked here?'

Without any hesitation, she answers him,

'Yes, my Me Ma has!'

Somewhat mystified, he questions,

'Your Me Ma?'

Mia asserts, into their conversation,

'Well, I've heard all this over our afternoon Tea break, so I'm just going to get another look at my new things and put them away, while you two talk.'

Lora continues,

'My, Me Ma, is my Grandmother.'

'I don't believe, my Dear that I would know her by that name.'

Lora giggles, and says,

'No, I would guess not, her name was... I mean is Liza!'

'Liza! Yes, that name does sound somewhat familiar to me.'

Mia chimes in again,

'Okay, so now that you're all squared away on that, Marcus, I'd like to show you what I have bought!'

Marcus approaches Lora to see her out, at the doorway unseen by Mia; he extends his hand to her, secretly passing her a handsome tip from his Robe pocket.

'Really want to thank you, Lora, for being such a great help to Mia, today.'

She looks down at her closed hand, and gratefully responds,
'Any time, it's been my pleasure!'
Then lifts her hand slightly to him, as she whispers,
'And thank you, very much for this.'
'You will please, tell Liza... I mean your Me Ma, that Marcus says Hello.'
'I positively will!'
With that Marcus slowly closes the door, then turns to Mia, who's standing in front of the full length mirror holding up an item of her new wardrobe in front of herself. Marcus notes, regarding Lora,
'Seems like a really sweet kid.'
'Oh, yes, very!' Mia agrees, as she turns to him still holding up the item in front of her, which is a lovely silk lingerie, Lavender sleepwear set, and seductively inquires,
'So, my Love, how do you like this?'
'Very lovely, Lavender is a divine color for you to wear, an even a lovelier color for me to see you wearing!'
'My thoughts, precisely!'
Marcus reacts to her statement, with a raised eyebrow and a pleasant admiring smile on his lips.

Mia closes the Laptop, stands, with her Wine glass in hand, and takes herself a satisfying deep swallow, and proclaims,
"Okay, good, one more chapter written, that's enough for this evening!"
She walks over to the window to see what the Moon is looking like tonight, and has some melancholy thoughts,
Ah... Mystic, Connecticut, it seems like a million miles away now, but the memories are still close to my heart; my Mom, the Cliff House, and my Late Birth Father, Michael Valli of which I never really knew, while he was living, that is. I have almost forgotten that in reality, after all I am still and will always be Rachael Valli. I must never lose sight of my real identity, even though I have permanently changed my credentials and my appearance from a Brunette with Hazel eyes, to now being a Blond with Blue eyes.

She lets out a deep sigh, clears her mind, sits down by the window, simply to relax and leisurely savor the finishing of her delicious glass of Wine.

CHAPTER SIXTEEN

A<small>NGEL</small> F<small>INISHES</small> H<small>ER</small> second cup of Coffee from her lunch, and as she's placing the empty cup down on the table, her Cellphone vibrates. The caller ID shows, unavailable, despite that, she questioningly, but sternly answers it,

"Hello?"

A Female voice replies,

"Yes, Hello. Is this U.S. Marshal, Special Agent, Seraph?"

"Who, may I ask, is calling?"

"This is Officer Cooper, Officer Beth Cooper of the Salem, Massachusetts, Police; I now have the 'C & D' order, and am already at the location for the serving of it. When can you get here, and will you need the address?"

"I can be there right quick, and I do have the address, thank yah."

"Okay then, Marshal Seraph, see you soon."

"Yes, Officer, I'll be there, lickety-split."

With that the call is ended.

Within a few short, but tense moments, Officer Cooper hears the roar of a Motorcycle engine coming down the road, and it stops right in front of her squad car. Needless to say, she is somewhat astounded by what she observes. Angel pushes out the kickstand while removing her Helmet, hangs it on the handle bars, shakes out her long dark hair, fixes it into a pony tail, unlocks and dislodges her Shotgun from the front fork of her Bike, promptly dismounts, to be now standing on the sidewalk holding it by her side, in an at ease manner. Taking note of these actions of Angel's, this slightly tall and lovely, fair haired, Officer Cooper exits her patrol car to greet her and inform her that the Weapon she is holding should not be necessary. Angel defending her actions extends her hand to this Officer in a greeting fashion and replies,

"It's real nice to make your acquaintance, Officer Cooper, but in these here cases of the unknown, it is standard procedure to have a Weapon with you."

"And it's very nice to meet you, Marshal Seraph, and yes, I totally agree with you, but from what I see of your Weapon, as you call it, it's a little of an Overkill for serving a 'C and D' order. Wouldn't you say?"

"Please, Officer Cooper, yah can address me as Angel. And this here, Overkill Weapon, as you put it, has saved my life a mite more than a few times, in my line of work!"

"Well... ah... Angel, I really don't think you will need it, just a side arm should do. You do have one, right? And please do call me, Beth!"

With that, Angel in agreement, secures the Shotgun back to her Bike front fork, unlocks and opens one of the Saddlebags to procure herself the impressive side arm, of a Forty Five Magnum.

Observing this, Beth has a rhetorical questioning thought,

Good Lord, who am I with, the female version of Dirty Harry?

Officer Cooper just smiles at Angel and says,

"Okay, then, Angel, let's do this!"

Officer Cooper with the 'C and D,' order in her hand, leads the way up the front walk, to Ms. Normans' front door, with Angel close behind. She rings the bell and they hear from inside,

"Just a minute, I'm coming!"

What opens the door is a very old woman strangely dressed all in black, with an old looking broom in her hand, and greets them with,

"Yes, Ladies, what might you want with me?"

Officer Cooper speaks to her,

"Well, Ms. Norman I'm Officer Cooper and we've had reports of you being rather naughty!"

"Me naughty, Officer? In what way, may I ask?"

Officer Cooper explains it to her, and ends with,

"And if you do not stop, there will be some very unpleasant consequences for you."

"Well, I do believe that every day, should be Halloween, and that I should be giving out candy to all the lovely Children that pass by my house. And who, may I ask, is that woman standing behind you, Officer."

"That is Special Agent Seraph of the U.S. Marshal's department, all the way here from Washington DC."

With that being said, Angel presents her Badge and smiles wryly in recognition.

"Oh my Dears, you are serious about this, you are not just dressed up in costumes for trick or treat!"

Angel chimes in,

"Yes, we sure are very serious ma'am, and no, we are not dressed up in costumes for trick or treat, Beth, please give her the order and we can be on our way."

As Officer Cooper serves her the order, she adds,

"We will, be watching you, Ms. Norman, so do make sure you stop, because if you don't, I regretfully inform you that, you will be sorry!"

As they start to turn to leave, Angel stops, turns around to ask,

"Why, ma'am was you call 'en the Children, Hansel and Gretel?"

"Well, Ms. Seraph... ah, it's from, you know, the Story, I didn't have any other names to call them."

"My name is, Agent Seraph, and that, ma'am is where ya made your mistake, cause that's what had the Children's Parents a worryin' about your alleged intentions, so you best stop this givin' out of candy, right quick! Like Officer Cooper here says, or you're a gonna' be a mite sorry."

With a slight hesitation the old woman replies asking,

"Wouldn't you nice Ladies, like to come inside for a spot of Tea?"

But before they can decline her invite, the City's Resident Witch appears on the sidewalk at the beginning of the houses' walkway; Beth turns round and says to Ms. Norman,

"Thank you, but, we must be going; I do believe there is someone here, that wants to see you, so just maybe she'll, have that spot of Tea, with you."

Ms. Norman replies,

"Okay then, you two Ladies have yourselves a lovely day, and blessed be!"

They make their way to the sidewalk where Officer Cooper greets Salem's Resident Witch respectfully, and she responds,

"Have a blessed Day."

After Officer Beth Cooper, and Angel responds in kind. Angel signs the completion Police report on the hood of the Police car, then thanking one another with a handshake.

Angel now shakes her head in disappointment of another bogus case, briskly walks to her Bike, undoing her pony tail, puts her Magnum back securely in the saddlebag, mounts the Bike while putting on her Helmet, starts up the engine and makes her way back to her Hotel, thinking,

Just another one of them there dag-gum false alarms, but this one was not just false, it was downright ridiculous. Good thing for me that they pay me well. Like I informed Officer Cooper, I'll have the Washington Office, send Salem my report. It being such a long ride to Washington DC, I don't want to delay it, by goin' to the Salem Police Station, before I start my trip to submit my assignment reports and to be seein' my Beau, which makes it worth every mile. But first, one more restful night at the Hotel, then right after breakfast, I'll hit the road south to DC, to be in the company of my sweet Beau, Mr. Victor Vincent once again.

CHAPTER SEVENTEEN

MIA WHILE SAVORING her Wine, sits at the window having some thoughts about where the story in her manuscript is going next,

Okay, so, I will be writing the first Sex scene between Mia and Marcus, this being their first with each other. I myself not being very experienced in these matters, with only having Sex for my first time with Shane, my first real love, and then only with him, until we split, with me sending him away, to keep him safe from Malevolence. There is that saying about, 'You only hurt the ones you Love' and I'm pretty sure there isn't one that says, 'You only kill the ones you Love'.

In the midst of finishing her thoughts, she makes her way to be seated at the desk,

I'll give writing a love scene an earnest try, and see how it reads. Where's Marlena's' ghost when ya need her? I'd be willing to fathom a guess, that she'd be very good at wording this type of encounter. Okay, so, who should be seducing who, wait a tic! I'll have them more or less seducing each other, okay, so, here goes.

Now with her Wine glass close by, she opens her laptop, adjusts her chair, puts her fingers on the keys, and begins to, get to it. Just as she types the first letter of the first word a soft knock sounds on her door. With a slight huff, she stands and makes her way to the door asking curiously,

"Who is it?"

A pleasant, familiar voice comes from the other side,
"Ms. Har... I mean Mia, it's me, Benjamin."
She, being fairly agitated thinks, but not too surprised,
Benjamin, again.
She states in recognition of him and asks as she opens the door,
"Yes, Ben. What is it?"
With a friendly smile on his face, he states and asks of her,
"So very sorry if I'm disturbing you, but, I just had to ask you, do you like Pea Soup? Jeannie makes a really fab Pea Soup! It is so delish, it really is an awesome Pea Soup with the ham and the...!"
Mia raises her hand in a stop motion, cuts him off,
"Ben, Ben my Boy, I really do value your concern for me, I really do, but I truly don't like Pea Soup. Would there happen to be any more of that delicious Tomato left?"
"Nope, not a drop, told ya before, it goes furiously fast, around here!"
"All right then, I'm a little busy right now, but you let me know when there is some Tomato. Okay?"
"Okay! Yes! Will Do! You bet!"
"Thanks, Ben,"
She replies as she's slowly closing her door,
"Talk to you later. Okay? Bye now."
Ben's smile turns into a frown, as he turns round and slowly walks away from her door, and down the stairs.

Now back at the desk, she begins again.
Marcus removes his robe and begins to get dressed, as Mia turns to him, still holding up the Lavender coloured Silk Sleepwear Set in front of her, inviting questions and asking,
'So, do you really like this one?'
'Yes, Mia, my love, I really do, it is truly quite lovely!'
'Well, you hold that thought, and stop what you are doing, because I'll be right out.'
She sweetly instructs him, as she swiftly goes into the Bathroom.

Mia abruptly takes her hands off the keyboard, and leans back in her chair, thinking,

This is so, moderately reminiscent of my first intimate encounter with, Shane.

She lowers her head and forlornly murmurs his name,
"Shane."

Then, reluctantly rises from the desk chair, and slowly walks over to the window with the clear view of the Hudson River, to take notice that it's an overcast day, as she's wiping the tear from her cheek, she grabs her jacket and heads out and down the stairs to the Lobby. From the bottom of the staircase, she stops momentarily to address Michael with,

"Hello, Mike."

Michael, at his counter, without looking up from what he is doing, just raises his hand in recognition of her. She then hastily leaves the Lobby, to head over to the River for a stroll along the bank, in an effort to clear her mind, so as to continue with the writing of her Manuscript.

Angel arrives at the U.S. Marshal's Building at just around noon, for her debriefing appointment with Director Hughes, she waits outside his office in reception going over her reports for the last three months. The office attended Agent tells her it will be a little while before the Director can see her, he's on a rather important conference call and she will need to wait. So she understands and informs him that she will step out into the hallway to make a phone call. He moves to the door and opens it for her; she exits out to the hallway. Takes a seat and activates her cell phone.

"I'll be out to let you know when he is ready to see you."
The attended informs her.
"That will be just fine, thanks."
She reciprocates.
Finding the number she wants in her favourites and dials it.
A man's voice answers her call.

"Hello, Darlin'! Where are yah?"

"At the U.S. Marshal's Building waitin' to see the Director."

"Will yah be much longer?"

"Not too sure about that, Victor but I'll try to make it as quick as I can. Where are yah?"

"At the liquor store gettin' a bottle of your favourite Champagne, already have the room for us at the Liaison Hotel, room sixty nine, for the night."

"That's just great, I'll need to make one quick stop before I can come there. Okay?"

"Sure, Angel, I'll be waitin' in the room."

"Alright, but don't yawl fall asleep on me."

"Iffin I do, you know the best way to wake me."

"I believe I do, sure!"

"Alright then Vic, I'll be with yah just as soon as I can be. I do believe I'm being summoned in now, bye."

"Angel! Wait, what is it you need to do before coming here?"

The office waiting room door opens and then the attended informs her,

"Agent Seraph, the Director will see you now."

"Victor Darlin, yawl find out soon enough", I need to go now, bye."

"Thank you, Agent."

She responds as she walks by him and in.

The debriefing takes about ninety minutes. As Angel stands and hands him the reports folder he says,

"Angel, before you leave DC, please call in to the office to check on if there is a case we may need you for. Okay?"

"Of course I will, but I really would like to getta' going now."

"Ah, Victor is waiting?"

"Well, yeah."

"Thanks once again, you two have yourselves a good time."

Mia slowly, but surely, makes her way back to her room. Sits at the desk and slowly opens her laptop to once again get back to writing her manuscript.

CHAPTER EIGHTEEN

MIA, WITH HER head down, and her eyes closed, places her hands on the keys, she leisurely lifts her head, sensuously sighs and begins to type slowly.

Mia slowly emerges from the bathroom, to see Marcus' naked body facing away from her, half covered by the sheet. She softly makes her way over to what would be her side of the bed, Marcus moves slightly, but not enough that it wakes him, she gently slides in to spoon with him, he lets out a low murmur as she reaches over his hip and slowly fondles his cock, he opens his eyes as it becomes erect, as she gently kisses the back of his neck he lovingly utters,
'Mia.'
Before he can turn to her, she softly whispers in his ear,
'Marcus… does that, feel… good?'
'Yes, my sweet, very.'
As he slowly turns over to her, and begins to gently fondle one of her breasts, then puts his mouth on the other. She swoons with pleasure, as she re-engages his cock giving it a gentle squeeze. She proclaims,
'Oh, my love, I never imagined it would feel like this.'
'It's good… Mia?'
'Oh, my, yessss.'
'It can only get better!'
'Better?'

With her question, he moves up to her face and they engage in a deep passionate kiss,

'Yes, better!'

With that said, he slides down to her Pussy, and begins playing with it with his tongue.

Mia abruptly breaks off from her typing suddenly stands, goes to the table, pours a half glass of wine, and in one large gulp empties the glass. She then realizes, she is sweating, and her face is feeling hot, so goes to the bathroom to splash some water on her face. When she raises her face to the mirror to her surprise, her eye colour is red. She proclaims,

"What the…? It would seem that, my writing of their lovemaking effected me rather strongly. Bringing back my memories of when Shane and I had first made love."

Bringing the towel down and away from her face, to see that her eyes have returned to the blue of the contacts she wears to make them that colour instead of her usual colour of hazel. Angrily, she throws the damp towel into the sink and proclaims bitterly,

"Damn!"

She returns to the desk in the attempt to complete the scene, when there comes a knock at her door, as she rises to answer it, she thinks,

Oh, yes, right on cue, must be Ben.

And sure enough, it is. Opening the door, she says,

"Benjamin my boy, what can I do for you, now?"

"Well, Ms. Mia, it's not what you can do for me, it's… it's what I can do for, you."

"And just what is that?"

"Well, knowing how much you liked the Tomato Soup, I just wanted to tell you that it's on this evening's menu."

"Thanks Ben, I'll be down for dinner later."

"I'll make sure that they save you some. Okay?"

"Yes, Ben, thanks again see you later."

She closes the door, turns round and softly leans her back against it, sighs, and queries out loud,

"Will I ever get this Book finished, and then Published. Maybe I can get their love scene finish before dinner, not real nice to leave them hanging, without an Orgasm, it's the lease I can do for them, it will be her first time, should make sure they obtain bliss. I mean they can't be having Forplay all night. Or can they?"

With that said, she giggles, and returns to the desk, more determined to finish the chapter.

What Marcus was doing gave, to Mia a feeling she had never known before, for her having sex was a new experience for her. She had been taught to save herself for marriage, but that was an old way of thinking, she had found a man she truly loves, no matter what he is.

She catches her breath and reaches down to put her hand on each side of Marcus' head and she whispers,

'Marcus, come to me... now.'

'I will be coming, my sweet.'

His answer has a double meaning, as he moves up to her, at the same time gently making penetration. They become as one, and after about twenty minutes, she obtains bliss again, and so does he.

Mia, brusquely rolls back her chair away from the desk and declares,

"O my God! I just described, in detail, what Shane and I had experienced for our first time, together. I think I need some cold water again, although this time, I think a cold shower is needed.

Angel lifts the Liaison Hotel front desk phone, dials room sixty nine. It rings twice, and she hears it being lifted, and then fall to the floor. She also hears,

"Oh man, it slipped."

And then she hears,

"Hello?"

"Yes, hello... Mr. Vincent!"

"Yes, Angel, ma love, I'm a waitin' on yah, the Champagne is chilled, and a waitin' on yah, too!"

"Oh, yah, and you where chillen' too.

"No no, my love just restin' a bit for our night together, it has been a while for us, we have quite a bit of time to make up for. Just wanted to be up for this."

"You'd better be UP for this! I'm on ma way to the room now!"

CHAPTER NINETEEN

Angel, Makes Her way to the door of room number sixty nine and softly knocks, Victor states,

"Come on in, It's open!"

Angel slowly opens the door and says,

"Howdy… well, I'm here!"

"I can see that, an it does, make me mighty happy that yah are."

She notices Victor is beginning to open the Champagne, but she stops him by saying,

"That will need ta wait a bit, I've done me a little shoppin' for something I was a hopin' you'd, like so just give me a minute to freshen up and get comfortable."

"Sure, Hun, it can wait. So that's what you needed to stop to get, before comin' here?"

"Yup, just a little something to spice things up a mite!"

"Oh, Angel my love, you've always been spicy enough for my, likein'."

"I know, I just reckoned I'd add some more. Never can have enough spice for us Louisiana Ladies. Right?"

"I reckon that's true, we Atlanta men, do like things spicy, sometimes!"

With her little shopping bag in tow, she goes into the bathroom, and slowly closes the door saying,

"Be out real soon, Mr. Vincent. Yawl be patient, now."

"I'll be waitin, with baited breath."

While he's waiting he calls down to the Hotel kitchen to put in an order for a late supper for two.

Victor, wearing no more than his black silk dressing gown, stands at the window watching the sun starting to get low in the sky. He takes notice that the shadows are getting longer and that the sky is getting some red tones.

He reflects,

What a beautiful evening to be with the Woman I love, more than anything else in this here world, and I've seen quite a lot of our world, plus many beautiful things in my line of work, but none to compare to my Angel.

He believes she'll probably be coming out soon so he lowers the lighting in the room. And takes a seat in a chair, with a good view of the bathroom door. And sure enough, it begins to slowly open and he hears her sweet voice call to him,

"Vic my love, are yah ready for me?"

"Ready as I'd ever be, my sweet, Angel."

She emerges slowly, like a professional model dressed in very little; wearing high heels, and a white silk Bra and Panties, adorned by a large white sheer wrap used like a cover-up to be worn at the beach.

She stops in front of him and with one word she poses the question,

"Well?"

"You have me… breathless!"

She gently falls into his lap, where he crushes her to him, and they intensely engage in a very passionate kiss. As he rises up from the chair with her in his arms, placing her ever so gently on the turned downed bed, where her wrap fans out on the bed, making it look like she has wings. He straightens up, now looking down at her he announces,

"My beautiful Angel, I truly am in love with you!"

She reaches up to him as he unties his dressing gown, letting it fall to the floor, revealing his erection. Angel declares,

"Well, I'd have ta say I beleave my extra spice is workin'."

"It sure is!"

"I'm sure glad of that, for both of us, now come to me, Mr. Vincent, and show me just how much yah missed your, Angel."

"Oh, I'll come to you and I'll be a showin' yah, alright!"

He kneels onto the bed, Angel moves to his rock hard cock and begins to tease him with her tongue, he moans with pleasure, when she backs off, he leans down to intensely kiss her, as he fondles her breasts with one hand and her pussy with his other, as he begins to lay down on top of her, she reaches down to his cock, to insert it into her now wet pussy.

As they settle into the missionary position they proceed to fall into their well established intercourse rhythm, after about thirty minutes they achieve simultaneous bliss. Victor, now sodden with sweat, he gently rolls off her, then lays beside her, holding her hand, catching his breath.

After getting his breath, he announces,

"I hope that made you hungry because while you were getting ready, I called down for a late supper of all our favorites, to be brought to the room."

Eyeing the clock on the night table, he says,

"Should be comin', real soon, now."

"Oh, yes, I'm famished, I hope you didn't order any dessert, because as usual I'll be yours."

"You know it Babe! You're the sweetest thing in my life, ain't nothin' sweeta', to me."

"Well, I'm fixing on grabbing me a quick shower before that gets here."

"Yeah, good idea, I'll just put a note on the door, iffin they come while we're in the bathroom, telling them to leave the food in the room and I'll join yah, in that shower, iffin yah don't mind."

"Iffin I don't mind? I insist!"

She demands.

After a cold shower, Mia hastily dries off.

Seats herself at the window in her new red silk robe, when she suddenly realizes it's time to get dressed to go down for dinner. After applying a little makeup, and fixing her hair, she dresses quickly, into a few of her new clothing items, and then heads down to the dining room for some of that delicious Tomato Soup and a main course of some red meat.

After her delicious dinner, she goes out to stroll along the bank of the Hudson River, hoping to clear any thoughts of her time with Shane. As she is walking, listening to the peaceful sound of the water flowing by, she looks up at a beautiful full Moon, after noticing its reflection in the water, as she's staring at it, it takes on a red hue, immediately she thinks,

Red moon at night, Vampire's Delite.

Yeah, I know... not the exact saying, but as a writer, I'm self given the right to apply creative liberties. I do believe, it's time for a little stroll up to the main road, to visit the local Tavern again, perhaps to see what just might be on that menu, for me this evening. Like I claimed a while ago,

"If I can't have Love, I'll have Blood!"

CHAPTER TWENTY

MIA, MAKES HER way leisurely to the, 'Horseman' Tavern up on the main road and as usual there is a sports game on the television, so she takes a seat at the bar and orders a glass of red wine. Joe, the bartender puts it down in front of her and asks,

"Shall I run a tab for you, Miss, Ah?"

"Joe, it's Mia… my name is Mia."

From a gentleman sitting adjacent to her at the bar, comes,

"Ah, excuse me, Joe, is it?"

"Yes yes, it is, and you are going to have to wait your turn, I'm not quite finished with the young lady, yet."

"Well, that's just why I am intruding, you can put her wine on my tab."

Joe looks at Mia with an expression that asks the question, 'should I'?

Mia, answers his look, with a hand gesture of approval, then she addresses the man for his kindness,

"Why, thank you, sir, that's awful nice of you to do that."

"Names Richard, but most people just call me Richie or just Rich."

"And are you?"

"Am I what?"

"Rich!"

"No, not yet, but, I'm working hard at becoming it."

"Working?"

"Mmm, yeah, on the road selling machine parts."
"Sounds like a very dreary job."
"Well, yeah, it can be, but it has its perks."
"Perks?"
"Yeah, like passing through a small town like this and meeting a pretty young woman."
"So you think I'm pretty!"
"Well…"
She cuts him off,
"There's no need to answer that, it was a rhetorical question."
"I kinda' figured, but… um… yeah, so, might I make a bold suggestion, it being a really nice evening might we, you and I that is, take a moonlight walk, along the river."
"You can suggest, but I would insist on it!"
"Great, so whenever you're ready, I'm not at all interested in the game that they are all watching on the television. You just say the word and we're out of here, I really don't think anyone will notice or care about us being gone."
"Well, as soon as I'm finished with the wine you bought for me, I'll be ready to go, and yes it is, as my great grandfather would say, a 'Bella Luna' night."
"A 'Bella Luna' night… yeah, I like that."

As Mia finishes the last of her wine, Rich motions to Joe for him, to pay his bar tab, so they can leave.

As they exit the Tavern, Rich takes notice of the beautiful full moon.

"Oh, yeah, it is a lovely night!"
"Ah, Rich, did you what to drive down to the river?"
"Drive, no, I don't have a car with me, I travel on my business trips by train, I find it to be more intriguing, trains for me always add a measure of mystery to my trips."
"Okay, then, I guess we walk."

They walk along mostly in silence. Until they come to where they can see the river, Rich notes,

"Wow, the moon really looks cool reflecting in the water. Its almost hypnotizing. Don't you think, Mia?"

"I guess so, never really looked at it that way."

"When I stare at it, it's kind of undulating, and it's making me feel a little dizzy."

"Yeah, Richie, that's what water tense to do, here, let me hold on to you as to steady you, to help keep you from falling on your arss."

She holds onto him rather tightly, he moves in to try to kiss her, suddenly he hears something that makes him turn his head away, exposing his neck, with his face turned away, he is not able to see that her eyes have turned red, her eyeteeth have converted to fangs and her finger nails grow longer. She now, holding him even tighter sinks her long fangs into his neck, and within seconds he is swooning from the loss of blood, his body goes lip in her arms, she props him up against a tree so she's able to finish her Blood Passion feeding, and like she has before with her other victims, strips him of all identification, plus a small messenger bag and then rolls this lifeless body into the rapidly moving Hudson river, which quickly carries the body away. And also like before tosses his things in a few moments after him.

She moves to a clear place on the bank where she can see her reflection, and watches as her eyes color changes and her teeth and fingernails go back to normal. There is a small line of blood on her chin, she wipes it away with her finger and cleans it off in her mouth. With all her pleasures satisfied, and any evidence cleared up, she makes her way back to the Bed and Breakfast. On her short walk back, she thinks,

Might as well, get back to my manuscript, really would like to finish it up, and get it published.

As she's walking, she stops slightly turns her head and says,

"By the way Richie, I really should thank you for a lovely and nourishing evening."

Mia arrives in the B&B lobby to find Mike at the check in desk with his head down working on some papers, she inquisitively greets him,

"Hey, Mike what yeah working on so late?"

"Oh, good evening Mia, just some paperwork, the accountant is coming this week and he's going to be looking for this stuff. I really hate this part of the work."

"Yeah, I think I understand that, writing for work can be such a bummer."

"Unlike the kind of writing you're doing. And speaking of that, how is your novel coming along?"

"Good, I was just out, taking a break from it, had a little of what they call writer's block."

"Oh, I've heard of that. Isn't that when your imaginary friends stop talking to you, you are, writing fiction. Aren't you?"

"Yes, I am, and you're somewhat correct about the blockage stuff. But it's coming along."

"Good for you, So, Mia how was your little walk?"

"It was rather invigorating."

"Are you going to bed, now?"

"No, not at all, not yet, too soon, I tend to do my best writing, late at night, or in the early hours of the morning."

As she begins to make her way up the stairs she says,

"Hey, Mike, don't you stay up too late."

"Just long enough to get most of this done, you can be sure, then I'm off to my bed."

"Okay, Good night, see you in the morning."

"Yup, see you then Mia, good night."

CHAPTER TWENTY-ONE

After Victor Leaves Angel in the Hotel room, while she is finishing up her breakfast, she calls into the U.S. Marshal's office to see if they need her for any other cases right away.

"Good morning, U.S. Marshal's office Washington DC, how may I direct your call?"

"Yes, Good mornin', this is Special Agent Seraph, please, if you'd be so kind, and connect me to the Directors office, I'd be much obliged to yah."

"Yes Agent, right away."

"Hello, Director Hughes's office. Who, may I ask is calling?"

"Yes, please, it's Special Agent Seraph, I'd appreciate it iffin' you'd connect me to the Director, thank yah, very much!"

"Sorry Ms., he's in a meeting right now, shouldn't be long, it's a routine morning briefing."

"Thank yah, I'll hold."

While on hold, sipping her coffee and thinking,

I can just imagine what that briefing could be about, maybe some regular things, but there might be another wacko runnin' round somewhere, for me to catch. I hope not really, would like to get back to Baton Rouge for a little while, and see what my sister Gabrielle has been up to, and how my little dog Bandit is doing without me, for so long. She'd best be taking good care of him. Really love that little pal of mine, that Victor had given to me for my... um, last birthday.

"Hello, Agent,... Director Hughes will speak with you now."

"Good, Thank yah."

"Good morning, Angel how was your night and how is Victor?"

"My night, Sir, was very nice! And Victor is just fine, he had to go into the Smithsonian early this mornin', he had a shipment of artifacts arrivin' from somewhere in the East on an overnight flight, to be put on or added to a display, he always has to be there to administer those things. Told me, iffin' he could he'd see me fer lunch.

"That is wonderful, but there is something I need to discuss with you, Angel."

"Oh, don't yawl tell me, yawl has something fer me to take care of. Do yah?"

"Yes, I do, but as usual it's always at your discretion whether to take it on or not, and don't forget you have complete impunity in these matters. And, please, remember you are the best at what you do for us and the world."

Angel, stops to reflect,

Oh yah, impunity in your world, that I came here to protect, but not from where I come from, that I gave up for this world of yorn.

"Well, Angel, do you want to here want it is or what?"

"Yah mights well, go on an tell me, Director, Sir."

"Okay, well, my Assistant Director, Joseph Thurmond, received a call a few days ago, from a Police Captain up in Fredericton, New Brunswick about some weird happenings going on there, they are not too sure how to handle it, so they asked him if you could come and help them out on this one."

"That's in Canada! Right?"

"Yes, it is Angel, figured you'd know that."

"Well, I… never mind, what time should I be in to meet with your A.D.?"

"Hold on, let me find out."

"Okay."

While on hold, she pours herself another cup of coffee, and sits back to think,

Really never thought I'd be this busy down here, actually could use a partner sometimes, in these here doins'. Wait, what am a thinking, ain't

no one else that would want to give up what I did to do this, I mean Gabrille did follow me here, but not to help me, she's much to lovin' an carein' an trustin' for this kind of stuff, a little too much sometimes, fir her own good.

"Angel, you there?"

"Yah, I'm here, Sir."

"Okay, he says he can see you about three. That be good for you?"

"Yah, goin' ta havta' be I'd reckon, leastwise, now I can meet my Victor for lunch, before I come to meet with him."

Angel lets Victor know she is free to have lunch with him. Their lunch date is made and kept. She tells Victor about a new assignment, that she may have to take care of before heading home to Louisiana. He wishes her well, they kiss and she heads to the U.S. Marshal's office for her meeting with Assistant Director, Joseph Thurmond.

Arriving at the A D's office, she is let into have a seat for a short wait. Assistant Director, Thurmond enters and circles his desk to take his seat announcing,

"Agent Seraph... I mean Angel, it is good to see you."

"Well, I'd reckon, it's good to be seen!"

"Shall we get right to it?"

Thurmond says as he reaches over his desk to hand her the case file. She leans forward to receive it and then sits back to give it a look. Not long after looking at it, she puts it down in her lap and looks up at him and proclaims,

"A Vampire! There's a person up there in Fredericton, New Brunswick, that's thinkin' their a Vampire!"

"Yes! Well, Angel that's precisely what the reports says, but that's not what is the disturbing part, the fact that they have a few injured and one dead victim is the thing that makes them need your help."

"Okay, I'll go on up there, and see bout it. When can I leave?"

He opens the middle drawer of his desk, takes out a packet, and hands it to her saying,

"Here is your voucher for one of our U.S. Marshal's jets to fly you up there, it will be cleared to leave at eight tonight."

"Oh, Sir, you knew I'd take this assignment?"
"Well, I had a hunch you would."
She smiles at him, as she takes the voucher, answering him with,
"Well, you just had yourself a hunch, did yah!"
All he can say is,
"Well."

With that, she leaves the office to get herself ready for this trip. She will need to have the bike loaded onto the plane's cargo hold, for the trip, with that done, she boards and settles in for the flight.

CHAPTER TWENTY-TWO

MIA SITTING AT the desk in her room, a little too wired for sleep, opens her Laptop, and questions,
"Now, let me see, where was I?"
She takes a sip of wine,
"Ah, yes, I remember now!"

In a house down the road from the safe house, after dinner, Tom is in the gun shed, cleaning the hunting guns, as Frank enters and proclaims,
'Tom, that was a good supper tonight, and by the way, we're out of ammo, and we don't have any lead left to make any.'
'Yup, well, we do need some fresh game for ourselves and the store behind the safe house, you're going to have to use the silver we have to make some. So that come morning, we can go hunting. I'll fire up the furnace, while you go get the silver we need to be melted.'
They work late into the night, producing what they need for their hunting at dawn.
They rise early, and dress in their hunting attire. Slowly and stealthily they move threw the wood, making not a sound.

Mia awakes first, she's feeling rather hungry after a night of love making. Marcus is sleeping very soundly, so she, ever so gently, slips out of bed, quietly gets herself dressed, to make her way down to the kitchen and get some coffee, and something to eat. In the kitchen the cook offers her breakfast, but she only wants toast and coffee, which she has and then returns to her room to find that Marcus is up and awake. Mia gives him a kiss and asks,

'Marcus, my love, are you hungry, would you like some breakfast?'

'Yes, my sweet, but not the kind you would have. I do have a hunger this morning.'

'I think I know what you mean, it has been a while for you, Marcus.'

'Yes, it has, I need to go out this morning and find a…'

Mia quickly interrupts him,

'Please, don't say it, just go do what you must, and please be careful.'

'I will, I should not be long.'

He dresses, in the only shirt he has left, that is clean.

Mia takes note of the color of it, and questions,

'Marcus should you be wearing that color?'

'Mia, you worry way too much, this brown one is the only one I have clean right at the moment.'

'Marcus, shouldn't you be wearing a bright color so that you will not be mistaken for an animal?'

'Mia, I must protest, you do worry too much, I'll be fine how could anyone mistake me for an animal!'

'Well, my love don't say I didn't warn you!'

'Duly noted, my love. Now I must go, get a small caliber rifle, be back soon.'

With a mutual kiss, he takes his leave of her.

In the thickly wooded area on this early dawn, Tom and Frank are on the trail, to the clearing, tracking what they believe is a large Buck.

From the opposite direction, Marcus is making his approach to this same clearing where he has, in the past, found large male deer for his blood feedings and to supply meat for the store at the safe house. As he circles slowly and stealthily in the thick bushes that surround this clearing, waiting patiently for his quarry to show itself.

'Tom, look on the other side of the clearing, I think I see something moving.'

'Let me see, Frank, yes yes, I think you're right there is something moving over there, I can just make it out through the bushes, and it appears to be the right color for it to be a Buck.'

Tom takes up his gun and aims it at the figure in the thicket, and so does Frank, and they fire simultaneously. At that instant a large Buck not too far from them, is startled and runs pass them. They both look at each other and nervously ask at the same time.

'*What the heck, did we just shoot?*'

Suddenly there is a knock at her door, she closes the Laptop, goes to the door and softly asks,

"Who is it?"

"Mia, it's me Ben, I noticed a light at the bottom of your door, and figured you were working late on your book, and thought you might like some coffee, so I have it here for you."

She opens the door, Ben hands her the tray and she says,

"Thanks, I really can use this right about now, you sure do take good care of me, Benjamin."

"Well, this is, a full service Bed and Breakfast, and we do care about our resident author."

"Oh, Ben you're too kind, thanks, now get yourself home and off to bed, I do believe you have school in the morning."

"Yup, I do, so good night, see you tomorrow."

"Yes, my boy, see you then."

She closes her door, takes her coffee to the chair by the window and somberly stares out at the moon's reflection in the river.

CHAPTER TWENTY-THREE

ANGEL RELAXED ON the jet plane while she reads over the case file, included with it now is her open ended reservation at the Delta Hotel in Fredericton and a hand written note that she also has an appointment with Police Captain Dupree, at ten in the morning at the Fredericton police station.

As she waits on the airport Tarmac for the Cargo hold ramp to be opened, to be able to get her motorcycle out, she inquires to one of the attendants about where the nearest Tim Horton's coffee shop is to the Delta Hotel. She is told, and files the info away for tomorrow morning, for before her meeting with Captain Dupree.

She drives to the Hotel and gets checked in, also orders some coffee from room service. While having a cup with a complementary croissant. She once again goes over the details of the case file. Feeling rather fatigued she changes for bed, lies down and no sooner falls off to sleep.

The wake up call, she asked for comes precisely at eight AM. Rising, she dresses in her riding attire, at the front desk, she gets directions to the nearest Tim Horton's coffee shop. Pulling up to park the bike a few people outside take notice of her and her very unique black and purple Harley Davison Motorcycle.

As she enters, quite a few patrons take notice of her, one patron in particular becomes very curious about her and has a strong feeling to approach her, but not for personal reasons, but for total professional reasons. For you see, this regular customer is a local radio personality who sees an opportunity for a very interesting interview for his show. He waits for her to have a seat, and with his coffee in hand, goes to her table and politely introduces himself saying,

"Good morning, and welcome to Fredericton, New Brunswick!"

"Well, Sir, thank yawl and good mornin' to yah also. Who, might I be asking, yawl is?"

"Of course you can, I'm Greg Gilbert, a local talk show radio deejay, I have a weekly show in which I do recorded interviews that get aired on a later date, with mostly people connected to movies, or music, but with you I'd gladly make an exception, unless you are a performer of some kind, which would not be an exception."

"No, I ain't no public performer, I'm afraid, what I am is rather confidential, as a fact."

"What, like, secret service, the CIA or the FBI?"

"No No, Sir, not quite those agencies!"

She gestures for him to have a seat, and as he does he asks,

"Can you tell me who you are, or is it too much of a secret?"

"Well, I reckon I can tell ya my name, but what I am and what I exactly do, I just might not be able to be tellin'."

He looks at her with insatiable curiosity and just emits,

"Well, I'm all ears, Miss!"

"Okay, Sir, so my name is, Angel Seraph, I'm a special agent with the United States of America's Marshals department, I've been liaisoned to your local police department to help 'em with a case."

"Really, that sounds very interesting. Can you tell me any more than that?"

"Fraid not for now, but just might be after the case is closed, I just might be able to oblige yah."

"Is it a… ah… oh, never mind, you probably can't say anything more right now?"

"No, I cant', must be gettin' along now, but iffin you can give me a contact number and iffin I have the time I'll call yawl, before I head back to the States, to do a recorded interview for your radio show. That is, what you are a wantin', ain't it?"

"Oh… yes… it is, please, here is the number, call me if you can do the interview, we can do it over the phone, right from your hotel room."

As she makes her exit with Gregs contact number, she declares,

"Well, Sir, like I said, iffin I have the time, yawl be a hearing from me."

She leaves and Greg thinks,

"Wow, it'd be great to have someone like her do an interview for my show, and that southern accent of her's is killer, I love it!"

Angel arrives at the police station right on time for the briefing meeting with Captain Dupree, for the case. As she enters his office, he stands and greets her,

"Please Agent Seraph, have a seat and I'll give you an update on the case." As he opens the case file he begins,

"Well, let me see now, we recently acquired information where the perpetrator has been seen coming, and going from." He hands her a sheet of paper and continues,

"Here's the address, and a modest map of the area, it's a run down section of the city, many abandoned buildings and a few houses, also."

"Sounds to me, like the kinda' place someone like that would likely hide out in. Captin' the report doesn't say if this is a man or woman."

"Yeah, I know we just this morning, found that out. We now strongly believe, but not are absolutely sure, that it's a woman. But please don't ask me why, of all the vague descriptions we've ever have of this person, they are always very well covered up, in a dark hooded cloak."

"Well, Sir, iffin' that is all you have for me, I reckon I'll go apprehend this person, and bring them in for you to prosecute."

She leaves the station to do some recon, of the location in the daylight, getting a mental picture of the abandoned house that this person is supposedly using, and of the neighborhood, so when she comes back at night, she'll know her way around. Riding back to the hotel to await nightfall, she has some pleasant thoughts of her time spent with her Beau, Victor, in Washington DC. Her plan now is to have some dinner, rest up, and then as fast as possible get this person, to close this case promptly, seeing that she wants to get home soon to check on things there.

After a nice dinner at a nearby restaurant, back at her room, she dresses for this mission, at her bike in the hotel garage, she checks all her weapons and ammo, hoping she really won't need to use them. After all, she has brought down, perps, without firing a shot, before. She rides in the area, and as she slowly passes the house, noticing someone dressed in a dark hooded cloak leaving it. Parking the bike, and securing it, about two blocks away, she takes what she believes she will need, then walks to the house to lie in wait. After waiting about two hours she hears a commotion, it appears this alleged Vampire has brought its victim to the house.

From her hiding place observing as much as she could by the full moon light, the scene is of a woman, trying to seduce a young boy, she could tell this from their voices, she can see enough to know that this self professed Vampire is trying to bite the neck of its victim. Angel abruptly stands up from her hiding place, and calls out,

"Alright freeze right there, U.S. Marshal, acting for the local authorities, you are under arrest!"

The assailant leaves go of the victim, and makes an attempt to escape, Angel fires her shotgun into the ceiling, with the purpose of getting this person's attention, and it does the job of stopping this suspected Vampire in its tracks. She quickly moves in to grab this aggressor, and as she does, something falls out of its mouth, the light of the moon shining on it reveals it to be a set of fake fangs. Angel declares,

"Oh Yeah… had me a feelin' you weren't no more than a fake!"

She then has a quick thought,

Ain't met me a real one, as of yet.

She handcuffs this bogus Vampire to a radiator and goes quickly to get her bike, while riding back to the scene, she calls in for a pickup. Promptly, a police car shows up and takes over.

She tells them,

"Tell your Captin', I'll be at the station in the mornin' to give em' my report, good night."

And then she rides off into the night, back to her Hotel.

Now back in her room, in her comfortable sleeping attire, she makes a call to Mr. Greg Gilbert, to sadly inform him that because her work is of a clandestine nature, she would not be able to give him an interview that would have any real depth to it, and could get her some trouble with her employer. He understands and wishers her well.

She then calls the U.S. Marshal's private report line to give her account on the outcome of the case. The agent that takes down her statement, also informs her that Director Hughes, has made special arrangements with the pilots of their jet plane, that they are to fly her directly home to Louisiana at her convenience.

CHAPTER TWENTY-FOUR

MIA FINISHES HER coffee, puts the cup on the table beside her chair, stands up, and as she walks over to the desk where her laptop is, she thinks,

Well, finished with my coffee, and I'm not sleepy, so might as well complete my manuscript, so I can get it to the publisher in New York City, that I've been E-Mailing with, about publishing it.

As she opens the computer she says,

"Tragic… just so tragic, oh, yeah, let me see now."

Putting her fingers on the keys, she begins,

Mia looks at the clock and notices that it's almost noon, and Marcus is still not back from his hunting. She was worried, now she's concerned, earlier, she believes she heard the report of some rather loud gun fire, or maybe, she hopes, it was just the crack of lightning.

Deciding to investigate, she goes downstairs to talk to Janus. She finds him in the kitchen, talking with one of the human kitchen staff, she clears her throat to get his attention, he finishes the exchange then spins around and addresses her,

'Ah, Mia, what might I do for you, my dear?'

'Well, Mr. Janus I'm worried.'

'Please, Mia, just Janus will do. So tell me, dear, what is it that has you anxious, you know that no one here will ever harm you!'

'Oh, I know that Sir… I mean Janus, it's just that Marcus when out early this morning for what he called hunting and he's not back yet, I fear something tragic has happened.'

'Yes, please, let us go into the sitting room and I'll see what we can do for you about this. There are two brothers that live just down the road, they know the wooded hunting area very well, and I suppose I can call them to have them take a look around, maybe they can locate him, or at the very least find out if anything has happened to him.'

Mia puts her face in her hands and sobs,

'Oh, Janus if anything bad has happened to him I just don't know what I will do.'

He puts a hand on her shoulder to comfort her saying,

'Now now, my dear girl, I'm sure he's okay and will be found, and be back here safe and sound.'

'I truly hope, in my heart you are right.'

Janus makes the call to these brothers, Tom and Frank, that he spoke of, tells them about someone from the safe house is missing, so to make a search of the hunting woods and report back to him straight away, on whatever they find.

'Okay, now my dear Mia, I'll have the kitchen make you some tea. You really need to calm down, this may be nothing at all, you'll see, he most likely just wandered off to far, and found himself a little lost, the boys will find him I'm sure, and bring him back here.'

Mia answers him, stammering with tears in her eyes,

'I do do hope yo you are rig right about that, Sir… sorry I mean Janus.'

He hands her his handkerchief, saying,

'Come come now, my dear, he'll be just fine you'll see.'

Mia leans back in her chair stretches and yawns, starting to feel sleepy now, so she saves her work closes the laptop, goes to the bathroom to ready herself for bed.

She wakes at ten AM, dresses and goes down for some breakfast, she orders a coffee and a peach muffin, as she's buttering it, Mike comes over abruptly, sits down, and excitedly inquires,

"Good morning Mia. How you doing this morning?"

"I'm well. And you, Mike?"

"Oh, My! I'm just dandy!"

"What's got you in such a good mood?"

"Well, Jeannie's making a special cake for me… my favorite!"

"That is awesome! What's the occasion?"

"My Birthday is tomorrow!"

"Wow, that's… that's great… I think."

"It's really great, I've managed to make it through another year!"

"Yeah, Mike, and I would say, you have many more to go!"

"Thanks for that, but with good health, I'd hope."

"The party is tomorrow night and everyone is invited. I hope you will certainly attend!"

"Mike… of course, wouldn't miss it for the world!"

"Good, now you enjoy your muffin, see you later!"

"Yup, later, Birthday boy!"

As she's finishing up her muffin, and coffee an idea of how to finish the chapter comes to her, which should get her close to completing her first novel.

As she makes her way back to her room, she has an amusing thought,

I wonder just how old Mike is, but it really doesn't matter to me, so I will not ask.

In her room, she goes right to her laptop, and begins,

Tom and Frank search the woods, they finally go to where they fired at something on the other side of the clearing, that they thought was a Buck. Frank starts to enter the clearing, but Tom hesitates.

Frank turns round to Tom and says,

'Hey, come on.'

'Ah… Frank do we really have'ta look over there?'

'Yup… we really have'ta look over there and any place else he might or could be. Now come on!'

'Ah… Okay, but what if we find him… you know… ah?'

'Ah, what… dead? And we did it? I ain't thought that far ahead, just yet.'

'But, Frank, I don't wanta', go to jail!'

'Neither do I, so will you please, show some backbone and come on!'

They get to the place that they think the thing that they fired at was, but they don't see, any body of anything, all they see is some clothing; containing a brown shirt a pair of jeans and boots and a small caliber rifle. Frank leans down to pick up the clothing and the gun, and what they find under them is a shallow pile of ash.

Tom gets a little hysterical proclaiming,

'Frank, there, there's clothes, but there ain't no body, no blood, nothing, nothing but something that looks like ashes, I… I mean this is crazy nuts!'

'Okay, now, Tom please, calm down, I think we got one them Vampyre peoples, that lives in the safe house, this, I think, it's what the sun does to their kind, it must be, because we had to use the silver for ammo, I think they don't like it so much.'

'Yeah, so what do we tell this Janus guy?'

'Well, first, we get rid of these clothings, we'll burn them at the dump, long with the rest of the trash like we normally do. Okay, now, Tom here, take this stuff, we'll just keep the rifle, can always use another gun, now let's make us a beeline to the dump, and get these clothings all burned up. Then tomorrow we just tells em' we looked all over and didn't find anyone.'

They both hurry off, in the direction of the private town dump.

CHAPTER TWENTY-FIVE

ANGEL FINISHES HER second cup of coffee, as the U.S. Marshal's Jet plane, prepares for a landing at the Baton Rouge, Louisiana Metropolitan Airport, so once again she stands on the Tarmac waiting for the cargo door to open, so she can get her bike out. While she waits, she makes a call to her home to talk to her roommate, Gabrielle, she answers Angels' call after about four rings,

"Hello, Sis, you've landed, golly, that was a quick flight!"

"Yup, it was, and I gota' tell ya its good to be home once again. Everything ok at the place? How's my little buddy Bandit? Did he miss his Momma?"

"The place? Ah well, um, yeah the place, just fine, I reckon. I was just tidying up a bit when yawl called, and yes, Bandit always misses his Momma, but he always knows he has me to be here for em."

"Okay, Gabby, the cargo door is openin', have ta' be gettin' my bike out now, be home soon, bye."

Gabrielle hangs up, and gets back to cleaning up. As she's cleaning, she reflects about last night,

My little party last night, was a mite wilder, then I was expectin', well at lease nothin' got wrecked, exceptin' for me, my head is sure anuff a poundin', I thought we kind weren't' affected by alcohol. I didn't feel drunk, but, I've for sure gotta' hangover.

Gabrielle, just gets about finished with the cleaning, when the front door opens, as little Bandit, like a bullet, runs to it. Angel bends down, and he jumps into her arms, vigorously licking her face. She backs him away, lovingly stating,

"Hey, little buddy, stop that now, you're ruinin' your Momma's makeup! But your Momma, still loves yah though."

With that said, she gently places this black and white pug dog down, which has black around his eyes, making him look like he's wearing a mask, hence the name Bandit. Gabby comes walking down the hall to greet Angel, they hug with a mutual kiss on the cheek, Gabrielle affirms and questions,

"Good havin' ya back home. How was the trip this time, lots a crazies, that a needed killin'?"

"It's good ta be home, and you, of all of us, are a knowin', I'm not permitted, by the powers that agreed, to authorize me to be comin here, to be killin' anyone. Is there anythin' to eat in the place? am feelin' a mite hungry."

"Why sure nuff, there's some food left over from a the pa… I mean, the place I ordered from last night.

"Ordered from?"

"Yup, yah know, Ruby's Rib Shack. Got some of those ribs yah sure loves! I can just, warm em up a little for yawl. And, by the way Sis, that little buddy of yourn is one spoiled little doggy."

"Good, and well he should be, I'm a goin' to get unpacked now, and freshin' up a mite. Be right out."

As Angel enters the kitchen Gabby informs her and asks,

"These here ribs, is almost ready for yawl, and, by the way, yah did get to be wit…. I means, see Victor on this trip?"

"Good, I'm more hungry than I thought, and yes, Gabby, I did get to see, my Victor, oh, ya, did I ever!"

"Good, that's good."

"Okay, Girl, what yawl a meanin', by that?"

"What I'm a meanin' is, Sis, is purely now, it's a good thin' you got him to be helpen' yuh with relieven' any of them there tensions you a mite be a haven' in your job you is a doin', as you so oftin' is a sayin' to me, down here."

"Well, my dear, you's the only one, that is a knowin what I'm a meanin' by it."

"True, ain't that so true, yup, that's surely is, a right truth. Now ain't it?" Gabby states, with a rhetorical question, and continues, "Angel, my dear evangelical sister, will we, be a ever goin' back?"

"Now I reckon that's a right good question, but my dear, you shoulda' thought about that before you followed me down here."

"Yeah Yeah, Angel, I know'd that. But a will we?"

"My dear sweet Sister, I reckon you a mite be, but about me, not so sure. Now nuff, with all these here questions of yourn, let me at them Ribs!"

CHAPTER TWENTY-SIX

MIA DECIDES TO get some sleep before continuing with her writing.

At about ten in the morning, Mia's awakened by a soft knocking at her door, slowly getting out of bed, adorning herself with a robe, she makes her way to the door, thinking,
I can only imagine who this might be, has to be my little knight in his imaginary dented armor, Ben.
She ambiguously questions,
"Who's there, who is it, at my door?"
The answer comes with a voice, from the other side of the door, but not quite the one she assumed it would be.
"Mia its me, Mike, would you please open the door?"
A wave of concern comes over her, she quickly opens the door,
"Yes, Mike, this is… ah."
Now, seeing Mike standing in the hall with a Breakfast tray makes her quickly change what she was about to say to him.
"Um… ah… I mean good morning, and thank you."
"No need to thank me… this is all Ben, he just called in a few minutes ago, saying he would not be in today, and asked no, more like told, me to bring you this."
"Oh, Mike! He's such a sweetie. Sorry about this."
"It's quite all right, Mia, he's a good kid, with good intentions, and he has established quite a fondness for you."

"Yes, you could certainly say that, he does take good care of me."

"Maybe, just a little more than he should, but like I told you, Mia, if he gets to be a nuisance, just let me know."

As she takes the tray from him, she says,

"Thanks again Mike, and Ben, an annoyance, I can't believe he could, or would be that to me."

"Like I said, he's quite a sweetie, and you are too, Mike!

"Okay, now Mia, you enjoy your breakfast, I'll see you later."

After she's finished with her Breakfast tray, she decides to get back to her writing. At her desk, she begins,

Mia paces her room, wringing her hands, praying loudly,

'Marcus, oh my love Marcus, it's been three days now, where in heaven's name are you? I refuse to believe that you are dead or have left me.'

She decides to approach Janus again, maybe he can do more than he already has. She finds him and asks of him,

'Forgive me, Janus, but it's been three days and nothing. What do you think we should do now?'

"Well, Mia my dear, I'd give it at least a week, you must know by now, how long our kind can go without nourishment of any kind. He'll be back, please be patient.'

'That is, easier said than done, oh, I'm so sorry Janus, I'm just so worried about him, I love him.'

'I know that, and how hard this must be for you. But please have patients a little bit longer, and try to understand we live in a different way than your kind does.'

As she walks away from him she relates,

'I will try Janus, I will try.'

Another week goes by, and Marcus still has not shown up, Janus comforts her to wait longer. And as hard as it is, she tries, she begins to believe that he is gone, and will not be back.

Now, after two weeks of crying herself to sleep each night, she's just about ready to give in to the notion that he is gone and will not be

returning. When suddenly Janus asks her to come downstairs, he has something he needs to show her, an item that was found at the dump.

As she walks into the living room Janus instructs,

'Mia, please, have a seat and try to stay calm I have something to show you.'

He produces a very small piece of a brown shirt with some burn marks on it and asks of her,

'Mia, does this look like the color of the shirt Marcus was wearing the day he when out to hunt?'

She takes it and abruptly stands up and proclaims,

'I want to say no, but... it does look like it. So want does this mean? That he was, burned to death?'

Janus answers her,

'No, only that this shirt, if it is or was his was burnt, there's no evidence that he was wearing it, when it was burned.'

'Janus, I'm sorry but, I've had enough, I want the keys to the car we came here in, I'm going back to the life I had before I met Marcus, but if he should show please contact me, you have what you need to do that.'

As he hands her the keys, he pleads,

'Mia, please, I ask you one more time...'

Before he can finish she cuts him off, hugs him, saying,

'Janus, no, I'm going up to pack up right now, and leave! Thank you for everything.'

Janus watches from the front door as Mia drives down the road and out of sight. The End.

"Wow, it's done, completed, finished, didn't think I'd ever get it done. Now to contact the publisher and send it in."

She closes the Laptop as she rises from her chair, to fill her wine glass to do a ceremonial toast to her accomplishment.

"This calls for a little fun tonight, that is, my extraordinary, kind of fun."

CHAPTER TWENTY-SEVEN

Angel Resolves To, take a week or so just to relax, and spend some down time with Gabrielle and her little dog Bandit. She regularly has been in touch with the main headquarters of the U.S. Marshals Department, in Washington, DC, and with Victor, urging him to come to Baton Rouge, to spend some time with her there, but he just can't get any time off, at the moment, so he sorrowfully must decline her invite.

On a beautiful sunny day Angel, Gabrielle and Bandit once again lounge on the deck of her Condo sipping on some home made Mint Juleps, Gabrielle has a question,

"Angel, do yah needs to call in like, everyday?"

"Yes, or they call me, but iffin it's an assignment, they will text me to call in to get the details, then like always I must be a goin'."

"Do yah always have'ta go?"

"No, not always but it's what they pay me for. I reckon yah do like this lifestyle yawl been a living? I mean it don't matter where yawl are from, or who you really are, to live here yawl, need money!"

"Yeah, I knows it."

"Then, why yah even a troubling to be asken' me that?"

"Just asken' is all, I misses and worrys about my sister, when she's away."

"Thems is sweet notions, and all, but yah knows darn well, I can take care of myself."

"Yeah, I knows that, too. But, I still worrys about yah."

"I know that, and I loves yah for it."

"So, please, yeah should just a stop yah worryin', now please get me a refill and make sure my little bandit has water in his bowl."

Without any more questions, Gabrielle accommodates her requests.

After about ten days of leisure time, Angel gets a text message telling her that there is a case they need her to handle. She is somewhat happy to receive this text because she's getting a little antsy just lying around doing nothing. She makes the call to the U.S. Marshal's Washington, DC Office and speaks to Director Hughes about the assignment.

He informs her,

"Angel, this assignment's location is in Tallahassee, Florida, an escaped convict, who was cornered in an abandoned house, came running out yelling that there was a Werewolf, living in the house. I will send you the address in a text. Please, take care of this as soon as possible. I'm also sending you an E-Mail with all the details. I will contact the pilot on duty for you to be picked up, and flown to Tallahassee, please call him also and let him know when you will want to go, but please make it soon! And yes, and when you have landed call me."

She answers,

"Yes, Sir, sure will do. Will be a leaving for Tallahassee, just as soon as the plane arrives, at the airport."

"Good, talk with you later."

On the flight, she reads the E-Mail with the details and thinks,

A Werewolf, really? Another crazy most likely thinkin' their one, when yawls they really needs is a shave and a haircut.

Once again as usual, she waits on the tarmac for the cargo hold ramp to open so she can get her bike out.

She contacts the local U.S. Marshal's office to request for at least two agents to meet her at the location, they concur.

Now at the location of this incident, she tells them, to just let her handle it alone, she makes her way into this abandoned house, fully armed, and ready for, just about anything, it's dimly lit, she enters a room that at one time must have been a lavish living room, suddenly something jumps onto her back, she swiftly reaches back, grabs what it is, crouches down, to flip it over her head, this thing lands on the floor losing its breath, she quickly straightens up placing her foot on its throat, it looks up at her, shows its teeth, and growls. With her shotgun against its forehead, she says,

"You a growlin', at me?"

In a garbled voice it answers,

"Jush… Just figured to scares, yah a mite."

"Is that a southern accent, I detect? So, I'm supposen' yah homeless."

She slowly removes her shotgun from his forehead, and her foot from his throat, and orders him,

"Now be a good little wolfy, rollover an put your hands behind your back."

He complies, she then handcuffs him, grabs his arm, and pulls him up to a standing position. She coaxes him to the front door, where they step out into the sunlight. The two Agents who were waiting outside on the street, come to her aid, by taking this person, and placing him in the back seat of their car.

Angel thinks,

Just another one of them there bogus cases, like I always say, it sure is a good thing they pay me well, whether it's for real or not.

"Thank yah, Agents, but this here one don't needs prison, he needs a docta! And some place to be livin', from what his a wearin', I'd be sayin he's a homeless Veteran. I'll head back to the office now to make out my report, I'm suppose en' I'll see you two there."

Angel drives off. The two Agents in the car look at one another and one of them proclaims,

"Now that, is a woman with balls!"

The other ads,

"Yeah, sure wouldn't want to cross her."

After she completes her report, and the debriefing is over, she makes a call to the Washington, DC, U.S. Marshal's Office to speak to Director Hughes.

"Director before I leave here, is there anything you need me for?"

"Well, Angel I don't have anything for you right away, a report came in, not too far from where you are. I need to check it out before I send you there, so just sit tight, I will contact you as soon as I have something more on it."

Angel hangs up and thinks,

Sit tight, I'm not that far away from Atlanta, maybe, just maybe, I should find out if Vic is home?

CHAPTER TWENTY-EIGHT

THE CLIFF HOUSE on Thirty Cedar Lane, in the beautiful waterfront town of Mystic, once more stands unoccupied.

A vehicle pulls up in front and parks on the street, the occupant just sits in their car, staring up at it, as if they are waiting for someone or something. A few minutes later, another vehicle shows up, parks behind the first one, this person exits their car and walks to the driver's door of the first car. Now, that driver exits and says,

"Thanks, Carmella for coming, I just don't know what I should do with this house, I was hoping you could help me decide on what I should do with it."

"Well, Mina, I'll be glad to help you in any way I can, not very sure in what way I could be, but…"

"Mella, I will welcome anything you could or can do to be of help with this."

"Mina, the truth is, with your Daughter Rachael, among the missing, you may now be, the caretaker, but not the legal owner, I suppose."

"Oh, but yes I am!"

"You are?"

Just then they both stop, and looking inquisitively at each other, they hear what sounds like a Motor Scooter coming down the road. And sure enough, as it appears over the low rise in the road, it is a person on a Motor Scooter. It is Rachaels' best friend Lucy, still using Rachaels' Motor Scooter that she had given to her for a birthday present. She pulls up to them, stops, dismounts and greets them with,

"Hello Ladies, its so fetch to finally see someone here at the Cliff House, most of the times when I do a ride-by, there ain't a soul to be seen, except of course, for the people the live in the other houses."

Mina addresses her,

"Well, young lady its very nice to see you. Where have you been? You know you could have come by my house anytime."

Carmella chimes in,

"It's Lucy right? I remember you, you were like Rachael's shadow."

"Not just, like, I was her shadow, but now, I'm just a shadow without a body, I really do miss her," She hangs her head and continues, "And to answer your question. Mrs. D., I'm attending college, so most of my time I'm there. But when I do get back around here, I cruise by, just to see. I ain't had the nerve to go up, and ring the bell or knock at the door."

Both Carmella, and Mina announce concurrently,

"We all miss her, Lucy!"

Lucy adds and questions,

"I still can't believe she's.... So what up, is it. You ladies, have going on here?"

"I asked Mella, to meet me here to help me decide what I should do with the house."

"Wait, Mina, you were saying that, you do own it."

"Yes, I was saying, a while ago, Rachael had me sign a legal document, that my husband Joseph drew up, him being a lawyer, he would make it a legal documentation, this document states that if she disappeared for more than a month the ownership would go to me, her Mother, so now I feel strongly the need to do something with it."

"But, wait, Mrs. D., just what if she's like not, like not you know? And she comes back."

"My dear Lucy, always the optimistic one, my dear sweet Lucy, she's not coming back, I need to do something with this house sooner or later and I'd really rather sooner, than later."

Lucy gives a suggestion,

"Okay, then you could, just give it to me!"

Both Mella, and Mina laugh.

Mia proclaims,

"Okay, now, yeah, let's be serious about this."

Lucy cuts in,

"But I was, being…!"

Mina cuts Lucy off and turns to Carmella asking,

"Mella, do you have any ideas? Would you, want it back?"

"Thank you Mina, by no means would I, want it back!"

"But you grew up here, it's your family home!"

"Exactly the reason why, I don't want it now and didn't want it then, when my Dad died, I had always told him to give it to my son, his grandson, Michael, for he has and had good memories here, I didn't. As a matter of fact, I couldn't wait to leave this house."

"Why… I mean…"

"Mina, my why, is rather personal, let me just say my overbearing Mother, and I never saw things eye to eye, about anything, it was a horrible existence for me growing up, so as soon as I could I left, and never wanted to come back here, even after my Mother passed. In the end, my Dad understood and loved me, and I always loved him, most likely why he became very close with my son, Michael. So there you have it, Mina and Lucy, forgive me, I'm sorry, but that is the whole horrid story. And speaking of unpleasant stories, what ever happen to Marlena Varlino? She owned and lived in it with her family for a while, and then all of a sudden she was gone!"

Mina reacts,

"Well, that is to this day still a mystery, this house seems to have a life of its own! So, Lucy, do you still want it?"

"No! I'm now like, believing I changed my mind."

"I thought so."

"Okay, it's been nice seeing you both, but I have to be going now, it's a long ride home for me."

"But Mella, what about the house, what should I do with it?"

As Mella walks to her car to leave, she declares,

"Mina, do whatever you feel; live in it, sell it, have it torn down, heck, give it to Lucy, I don't care. Goodbye, both of you be well."

They both wish her well, as they wave goodbye.

Lucy then turns to Mina and requests,

"Mrs. D., can we go in, to have one last look around?"

Mina, is hesitant for a moment, before answering,

"Okay… yes… Lucy. Why not? Come on!"

CHAPTER TWENTY-NINE

MIA DECIDES TO make a social night of it, in celebration of the completion of her first novel. She will contact the BriteFire Publishing Company in New York City, early tomorrow and then E-Mail it to them. She is dressed quite alluring in a cream colored silk blouse and a short black pleated silk skirt, while applying her makeup, she leans in close to the mirror and asks,

"Hey... Racheal, you still in there, aren't you? I will find, a way to bring you back! Mia is a pretty name, but Rachael is a better one, after all it's my real one. And it is, the female version of my real late Fathers name, Michael."

After pouring herself and enjoying a glass of wine.

She heads down to the lobby to ask Mike something. Fortunately for her, he is as typically, at the registration counter, working on something. She slowly approaches him, greets him and asks with a big smile,

"Good evening Mike, can you please, tell me where I can get a drink around here besides, the 'Horseman' Tavern?"

"Certainly, my dear, there is another place nearby. Wasn't it in with the Brochures here on the counter, wait," as he looks within the pile not seeing one he continues, "I'm sorry, those are all out, will need to get some more. But first I want to know, what's up with the big smile you're wearing on your face?"

"Well, Mike, believe it or not, I just finished my first novel, and I will be sending it in for publication tomorrow, so I'm going out tonight to celebrate a little."

"Well then, tomorrow night we can have… no, we will have, a small party right here for you, I'll tell Jeannie to bake a special cake for it, so we can help you celebrate this wonderful accomplishment of yours. I know Ben will be so happy for you!"

"That will be very nice of all of you to do that for me, but Mike for now, please, tell me about this place you know of."

"Yes, my dear, its on the river road just a little ways from here, you will spot it on the right, there's a large, well lit sign, many people that are passing through on business stop there for a short rest and refreshment, before continuing on to their destination. Although the locals go there for special occasions and stuff, they even have a hall you can rent for large parties, my sister Jeannie took me there for my Sixty Fifth Birthday, it's a real nice place, and the way you are dressed this evening is just right for this spot, for you to have your solitary celebration, I would say."

Mia leaning on the counter with her chin in her hand, listening patiently to all he has to say, lifts her head to interrupt him and questioningly states,

"Okay, so Mike, just what is it that is written on this, well lit sign? You are going to tell me, right?"

"Oh yeah, was getting' to that, it says, 'Andrea's La' Bistro on the Hudson', it's quite the swanky place,

"Well, for my intentions, that sounds just perfect. Thanks Mike, I'll catch you later."

"Yes, see you later, have fun!"

Mia parks her car in the restaurant lot, checks on her makeup in the rearview mirror, winks in approval and exits the car. Closes the door, turns round to get a look at her reflection in the car window, shifts her clothing a little, checks her hair and says softly,

"Looking good, Rach... I mean Mia, oh no, that was a slip-up, I'd not what that to happen, for someone to hear, they might think I'm a psycho or something."

With a deep breath of confidence, she makes her way to the door, the Doorman opens the door saying,

"Good evening, Miss! Welcome to Andrea's La' Bistro on the Hudson."

She thanks him, slowly enters into the lobby, to be greeted by the Maitre' d, which addresses her with an inquiry,

"Good evening, Ms., does one have a reservation for dinner with us this evening?"

"Well, no, wasn't aware that I would need one."

"That will be fine, I believe I can accommodate you with a table. Will you be dining with us introvertly this evening, Ms.?"

"Yes, I will, thank you, but if possible Sir, if you please, a table near the lounge area."

"We do have a few intimate tables right in the lounge, would one of those, do for you, Ms.?"

"That would be absolutely splendid, thank you kindly."

Now seated at her table, the wait person takes her drink order of a glass of Chardonnay. As she awaits her drink, she provocatively crosses her legs, making certain her goodies are slightly hidden, beneath her shot pleaded silk skirt, then proceeds to scan the room for tonights object, for her Blood Passion.

A youthful looking, handsome man seated at the bar, catches her eye. As if he can feel, her wandering eye falling upon him, he turns in her direction. Their eyes meet and she smiles, he returns the gesture. She slowly pushes the empty chair on the other side of her table out with her foot, as a seductive showing of an invite to join her. As he picks up his drink and moves off his seat to accommodate her invite, her wait person returns with her wine and they almost collide, he excuses himself, then quickly sits in the empty chair. As he sits, Mia's wait person, asks if she'd like something to eat from the menu, she answers with an order of shrimp cocktail, she and the wait person, then both look at her guest questioningly, he conceives what they are insinuating and looks up at the attendee and says,

"No, nothing for me, thank you. As the attendee walks away, he looks at her, placing his hand on his chest announcing,

"Jason! It's nice to meet… you… ah?"

She returns,

"Mia! It is nice to meet you also… Jason!"

They both laugh and concurrently quote,

"Yeah, 'Me Tarzan, you Jane' and they laugh even more. After their laughter dies down he states,

"Edgar Rice Burroughs."

"Excuse me. What?"

"The author, and creator of Tarzan!"

"Oh yes, Right."

They small talk, while Mia has her shrimp. He enlightens her, that he's on a business trip, just passing through Sleepy Hollow, from Toronto, Canada and will need to get the train tonight, bound for New York City.

She asks,

"How long before your train comes?"

He looks at his watch and the train schedule and answers,

"I figure, I've a couple of hours before I need to get a cab to the Station."

"Oh, Jason, I'd be glad to take you to the Station, my car is out in the restaurant parking lot."

"Great, that means I have even more time."

They make a little more small talk, as Mia finishes her order, Jason looks at his watch to see that the train should be at the Station in about twenty five minutes or so. He mentions this to Mia, and she inquires,

"How far is the Station, from here?"

"Ah, let me see, the cab ride here was about two minutes, so I'd say, It should be about the same to get back, to it."

"Good! Then we have time for a nice moonlit walk along the river. What do you say to that idea?"

"I'd say that's a great idea, and you can tell me all about your novel that is about to be published."

"Good, let's go!"

He motions to the wait person for his and her bill and pays both with cash. They rise, Jason grabs her jacket off the back of her chair and helps her put it on, they leave the restaurant, she pulls out of the lot headed for the Station. As they ride along the river road, she is on the look out for a clear place along the river bank for their walk. She spots what she feels is a good place and pulls over and parks, they get out, he makes mention of it being a beautiful night, she agrees, as they stroll along she tells him of her book. He suddenly interjects,

"Vampires! Really? Do you truly think they exist?"

"Well, it's hard to say that they don't, after all, from what I understand, no victim has lived to tell anyone, so there's a very good chance that they do. Now wouldn't you agree?"

As she's speaking, she turns round, and is walking backward in front of him to be able to see his face, she stops when her back comes up against a tree. He makes his move to try to steal a kiss, Mia without him noticing, kicks something into the water, he turns his head to see what it could be, so she once again takes advantage of the clear opening to the neck of her victim, that will not live to tell what happened, or catch his train.

Now back at the Riverside Bed and Breakfast, Mike states and asks her, as she walks up to the counter.

"So Mia your back! How did you like the place?"

"Liked it just fine, thanks for the tip, I'll see you in the morning."

"Yes, my dear, sleep well, and we will have a little party for you tomorrow night after dinner."

"If you say so Mike, Good night."

CHAPTER THIRTY

ANGEL DECIDES TO, maybe get herself a room in Tallahassee, and wait for either Victor, or the U.S. Marshal Director to contact her. But first, she'll go to a local coffee shop. While having her coffee, she gets a text from Victor telling her,

'I'm so sorry my love I'm out of the country right now.'

She texts him back saying that, she is sad he is not around, but understands and still loves him, he replies in kind. About a minute later she gets one from the Director,

'There is nothing going on close to where you are so you can just go home if you like. I can have our plane take you.'

Her answer is, that she will drive herself back to Baton Rouge on her bike.

After about three hours on the road, of her six hour trip, she makes a stop for something to eat, get refreshed and call Gabrielle to tell her that she's on her way home.

Another two more hours of driving, she feels she needs a rest stop, so she pulls into a Prime truck stop, to use the toilet facilities, as she comes back out to her bike, to find a small group of truckers standing around it, she walks up to them, roughly makes her way through them excusing herself, they reluctantly part the way for her to get through them to her bike. When they see, that it's a woman rider a few of them start to make cat calls, a rather large portentous looking, trucker wearing a Harley Davidson cap, steps forward from the group and they quiet down and stop. He seems to recognize her, and asks,

"Cuse me, ma'am, but ain't yawl U.S. Marshal Angel?"

"Yes, I sure am!" Do I know you?"

"Maybe not, but I sure nuff knows about you, I've seen you in action, and coulds never mistakin' this bike of yourin', its a beauty. You are the best at catching those crazies, thats thinkin theys supernatural things likes thems there Vampires, Werewolfs and the like. The names, Merle, and I reckon it's real mighty nice to actually meets yah."

"Well, Merle, it's real nice to meet yawl, and thanks for what yah did for me here, just thinken' there might be some trouble here with some of these here truckers.

"Oh, tweret nothen', they really did ant' means ya no harm, theys was just admiren' your bike, and was a little taken'-a-back by you being a mite handsome looking woman and all. Yawl, headed to, a job?"

"No, headed for home, just took care of one, back there in Florida."

"Yeah, so just about where's yer, home?"

"Louisiana!"

"Loosyanna! That's where I was borned and raised, my Granny still a livin's there, I's livin's in Texas now. Okay now, girl, yawl have yourself a real safe trip, home."

"I'm sure fixin' to, and thanks again."

She starts up the bike, puts on her helmet, and as she drives off, Merle waves goodbye, answering her, but she's out of earshot to be able to hear him,

"No problem, be safe, maybe we's be seein's yawl again sometimes real soon."

Angel arrives home with a big welcome from her dog Bandit. Not seeing Gabrielle, she hollers out to her,

"Hey oh, Gabby I'm home, safe and sound!"

Gabrielle hollers back,

"Hey, Sis, glad your back, I'm outs here, ons the deck."

"So what yawl been up to since I been gone?"

"Well, no one was round to hang with, so's I's been doing a little reading again."

Angel picks up one of the books and asks,

"You still readin' those Vampire stories?"

"Yup, sure, I just figures you catchs em, I'll reads about em.

"Well, Sis, that's just be fines, but yous do realize they's all nothing but fantasy an fiction, ain't fir sure come up against, a real one yet."

"Yup, I knows that, but I got's me an email from the book site I belongs to about a new one, comin out soon! And it's a soundin like, a real goodin!"

"Oh yeah, a goodin one hah? What's the title?"

"They says, it's supposed ta be 'Mystic Vampyres'."

"Oh my, sounds a mite scary!"

"Come on now, Angel, like you says, it ain't nothing but fantasy an fiction."

"Yeah well, Gabby, don't you ever get to believin' its anythin' exceptin' dag gum untrue stories."

"I won't. Cause inffin, anyone would know the truth, it's be my Sister Angel, this here worlds, awesome 'Vampire Hunter'!"

CHAPTER THIRTY-ONE

MIA WAKES AT about ten in the morning, just the right time to contact Ms. Able, at the BriteFire Publishing Office in New York City, to let her know that the manuscript for her first novel: 'Mystic Vampyres' is now complete and ready to be E-Mailed for the process of publication.

Conversing with Ms. Able about the text and a cover design, while they are speaking, she sends it off. Mia is reminded, once again, it will most likely take about a month or so, for it to be ready for her final approval, of the text, and the cover design. She has already signed the contract with them, and she understands the agreement and says,

"Thanks for all you've done so far, I'm excited and a little impatient about the whole process. But I guess all I can do now is wait."

"Yes, we will be in touch soon, but if you have any questions, please don't hesitate to call me."

"Will do, bye for now."

She hangs up, and begins to get ready to go down for breakfast. Dressed casually she heads downstairs. The first person she sees as she steps on the floor of the empty lobby is young Benjamin, feeling very excited for her, he proclaims,

"Well well, there she is, our so cool, soon to be Published Author!"

"Yes, Ben, and thanks for the introduction to," She looks around the lobby, "um, nobody, except you and me. But really, do appreciate your enthusiasm."

"So, Mia, how long before the book comes out? I'm dying to read it, really can't wait!

"Well, Ben, you've been so good to me. How's about I print out a copy for you to read in advance of the publication, which will take about a month or so I'm told, would you like that?"

"Would I! Yes oh yes, that would be so boss! Just about the most excellent thing any ones ever done for me!"

"Well then, Ben, I'll get to it right after breakfast."

After having a light breakfast, she makes the arrangement with Mike, to be able to send the manuscript to his printer, for that advance copy she promised to Ben for him to read. While it is printing, she'll have herself a relaxing stroll along the Hudson River Bank, really hoping that her novel will be somewhat of a success. As she leisurely meanders along, she can't help having memories of her life back in Mystic, she also ponders what has, or may happen, to the Cliff House, and also thinking about her Mother, Mina, Step-Brother, Mathew and Step-Dad, Joseph, and of course, her childhood ditzy pal Lucy, plus the thoughts of her real Father, Michael Valli hardly ever leave her mind. Then, suddenly a random curious notion erupts into her thoughts,

Will I ever see Shane again?

She doesn't like to profess to it, but, she reluctantly realizes, in her heart of hearts, she still has deep feelings of love for him, after all he is, and was, her first real love and lover. Her eyes start to well up, so she quickly puts anymore thoughts of him, her family or Mystic out of her mind, takes in a deep irregular breath, turns around and heads back to the Riverside Bed and Breakfast.

As she enters the lobby, Mike is signing in some new guests, he notices her enter, he points her out to them and excitedly informs these new Lodgers,

"Well, what a yah know, there she is now, right on cue, Ms. Mia Harkness, our soon to be published resident author!"

The women in this small group turn to see her and pose the question,

"Oh please, Ms. Harkness, you simply must, tell us about your novel, the title of it, of course, and when it will be available for us to read it, because we do have a book club, and are always on the look out for new books.

At this point, the men in the group go out to bring in the luggage, so now, Ben stands at the ready to help them get it to their rooms.

Mia enthusiastically, enlightens these ladies about her Vampyre novel, by giving them its title; 'Mystic Vampyres' and also a brief synopsis, then informing them that it should be available in print copies and E-book in about a month or so, from the BriteFire Publishing Company of New York City, and all the booksellers on the internet, also hopefully in book stores. Hearing what she tells them, these ladies get very excited, and consign to reading it just as soon as it becomes available to them.

One of the ladies asks,

"Will you be doing a book signing tour?"

She answers them,

"I would surely hope so, ladies!"

Another one of them chimes in with,

"We assuredly will be watching your Publishers' website for your signing tour schedule."

Mike politely interrupts by informing them that, it is time for them to go to their respective rooms to get settled in. They all agree and leave the lobby, goodbyes are exchanged by all, as they disperse. Mia leaves the lobby last and Mike reminds her by saying,

"Mia don't you forget about the congratulations party, we have planned for you this evening."

"Wouldn't want to miss that, not on your life or mine, Mike. What time will it be?"

"In the dining room around eight thirty, I believe, I'll be sending Benjamin up to your room to escort you down to the party."

"I'll be expecting him!"

The party goes off without a hitch, Jeannie made a beautiful three layer red velvet cake with vanilla frosting, and in keeping with the Vampire theme, she put a design of Vampires' Fangs on it, and she also baked a large chocolate sheet cake, likewise with vanilla frosting, sporting a design of an open book with a makeshift title page showing the title of the novel 'Mystic Vampyres', with the authors' name too.

Everyone, all the guests at the Inn, of course, was welcome, it is a come one, come all, occasion. Young Benjamin, feeling very special, went home early with the manuscript printout, so he could get started reading it.

In the morning, Ben comes happily bouncing into the lobby with the printout of the manuscript in tow, and a really big smile on his face. He briskly walks up to the counter puts it down, steps back to take his seat at his station, the lobby bench. Mike queries of Ben,

"So you read it all, in one night?"

"Yup, it was so bit-chin, couldn't put it down, had me rapt, almost felt like it really happened. And I feel so superior, to be the first person to get to read it before it goes out there to like, the whole wide world!"

"Ben, what'd I tell you about using that word, bit-chin around the Inn?

Ben puts his head down and softly answers,

"I'm sorry Mike, it slipped out, won't happen again."

"Please, see that it doesn't."

"Okay my boy, well, last night, my sister Jeannie happened to overhear about you being given, for yourself an advance printed copy, of Mia's manuscript to read, and claimed she'd really love to read it too!"

"Mike, I think you should really check that, with Mia. I don't want to be getting into trouble with her, so please, clear it with her first."

"Certainly will do that, Ben."

"Good! Mike, has she been down for breakfast?"

"No, haven't seen her as of yet, this morning, she should be down soon though."

Ben abruptly rises from the bench and starts pacing the lobby floor, announcing,

"Yeah yeah, real soon I hope, I'm so like pumped, to tell her how much I love her book!"

"Okay, my boy, I will have to insist that you're not going up to her room and bother her, so just sit and chill for now, try to be cool untill she gets down here."

Ben, reluctantly sits back down on the bench, crosses his legs, letting out a slight undertone grumble of,

"Girls, sorry I mean women, they take so long to get ready."

"Yes my boy, they sometimes do, so you just chill out now!"

Again, he grumbles under his breath.

Mike just goes about his morning business.

CHAPTER THIRTY-TWO

Mike Tells Benjamin to go up to Mia's room, just to tell her that a box from New York City has arrived for her.

Ben answers,

"Yes, I will Mike. What do you think it could be inside?"

"How the heck, would I know?"

"You could… like guess!"

"No, I can't, like guess, you just go up and tell Mia and she will come down to open it and then we will know, now go!"

With that said Ben races up to the second floor to her door, and knocks softly, announcing and asking,

"Mia its me, Ben. Are you up yet?"

He gets no reply, so he knocks a little harder, then stops to listen, he thinks he hears movement so he calls out again slightly louder,

"Mia its Ben. Are you awake?"

From inside he hears,

"I am now. What is it?"

"There's a box, from New York City been delivered this morning for you down in the lobby. Should I bring it up to you or do you want to come down and get it? Please, say you'll come down."

"I do need some breakfast, so I'll be down in a minute."

"Awesome, see you down there."

Ben excitedly comes back down to the lobby announcing,

"Mike, she's coming down, she's coming down, we're gonna see what's in the box!"

"Ben, I'm telling you, boy, one of these days you're going to bust a gut!"

As Ben starts looking the box over, he says,

"Mike, I just want to know what's in the box, you know you do too!"

"Yes, I do, but don't you go, shaking it, just might be something breakable in it."

"Darn, can't read who it's from, that part is all smudgy!"

"Yeah, I've seen that, it must have had something spilled on it, just sit down now, and wait for Mia."

"Yeah, okay, Mike, easy for you to say."

Just as Ben finally sits down, they both hear someone coming down the stairs.

"Is it her… is she here? I sure do hope it is her!"

"I also, sure do hope it is her, before you, bust a gut!"

Angel opens the door of her condo in Baton Rouge, drops her rucksack on the floor, and as usual her little dog Bandit comes running to her, she scoops him up and walks into the kitchen, where Gabrielle is making spaghetti sauce. Angel announces,

"Well, as yawl can see, and hear, Gabby, I'm back once again safe and sound!"

"Yup, and I'm sure glad of it, too."

"Why, yawl so glad to see me, Sis?"

"Always, I'm glad to see you back alive. What was this one, numba three in the last two months?"

"Yup, numba three, and just as phony as the last two was! What would I give to come up against a real, honest to goodness, no wait, not goodness, but a real supernatural perpetrator! Ain't hads me one, for quite a while now."

"Yah, when was the last real one yous had? Wait, was an' it the one a while back, down there in New Orleans, when you went ups' against, like three of em, that's been real looking and acting like Vampires. I means leastwise you told me theys had a couple of young girls, that they was about to bite on em, when yous came a bustin' in and took em down, real hard!"

"Yup, I'd a have ta say that was the one! Wow! Sis, yous got yourself a real good memory there. Yous writin a book or something on what I'm a doing?"

"No, but maybes', that's not a bad idea! What yah thinks?"

"Well, ah, let me see, what I thinks is it's a horribly really horrific idea! It could expose, who and what we both really is."

"Oh, come on now Sis, ain't no ones is a gonna believe the truth about who and what we really is, and from well, yous know wheres."

"Yup, Sis, and we needst to keep it that way whilst we're here."

"Okay, I gots yah! Hope yous is hungry, cause'in the pasta is a ready, so we's can sit's, and chow!"

"Yup, I reckon I am, and I do have me a like'in for your pasta sauce cookin!"

As they eat Angel asks Gabby,

"Speakin' of them there Vampires. Whens is that new book yous been wanten to read a comein' out?"

"Shoulds be available any day now! And I just cans wait, to gets me one, although I do believes the author, Mia Harkness, is a gonna be doing personal appearances for book signin's, if she is a gonna be doins that, I's can wait tell she comes round here."

"Okay Gabby that's good, and so's your pasta!"

"Thanks, Sis!"

No sooner does Mia put her feet on the lobby floor, when Ben suddenly jumps up, slaps his hand on the box, positioned on the registration counter, and proclaims excitedly.

"Here it is… here it is, open it Mia open it!"

"Yes, Mia, please come over here and open it, do, before Ben busts wide open!"

She comes to the counter and looks at the box, and declares,

"Well, I would guys, but I need something to…"

Before she can finish her statement, Ben takes from out of his pocket, his jack-knife, opens the blade and carefully hands it to her saying,

"Here you go, Mia, and please be careful, but hurry!"

Mia places the knife on the packing tape on the box, but stops and hands the knife to Mike requesting of him,

"Here you go Mike, you do the honors, please."

"Sure will," he begins to slowly cut the packing tape asking, "So, Mia, do you have any idea what is in here?"

"Well, guys the first clue is that it's from New York City."

Ben chimes in,

"We did see that, but the name of whom it's from is all smudgy like."

"Yes, Ben I noticed that too."

At that moment Mike gets the box open, and takes out some packing stuff to see what it is in the box, while Ben is stretching his neck, from behind Mike to get a look.

Mike looks at Mia, tips the box toward her and requests of her,

"Mia here, have yourself a look!"

Meanwhile, Ben is trying to see in the box saying,

"Let me see… let me… see!"

Mia requests of Mike,

"I'm much too nervous, please, Mike you take what it is out, for me!"

Mike quickly reaches in and comes up with one of the five copies of her new novel announcing proudly,

"It's "Mystic Vampyres' your new novel!"

Ben excitedly proclaims, loudly,

"This is so, so bit, um… I mean so fetch!"

CHAPTER THIRTY-THREE

M IA T AKES T WO copies of her new novel, 'Mystic Vampyres', from out of the box, takes the pen from the counter, opens one to the title page and signs it, hands it to Ben saying,

"Well, my young friend here is your very own personal signed copy, just for you."

She does the same, to the other, then hands it to Mike saying,

"And this one, Mike, is for you!"

"Well, Mia, if it's okay with you, I'd like to give it to Jeannie, she did so love reading the printout of it."

"Hey Mike its yours, to do what you wish with it,

plus I'd also like to leave one here with you Mike, for the Inn. To be read on loan, for employees and maybe even a guest."

"That is very nice of you to do, Mia!"

Ben excitedly agrees,

"It, it sure is, it's really a most rad thing!"

She hands Mike an unsigned copy. He responds,

"Okay, Mia, I'll put it on display high up here on the shelf behind me, where it can be seen by all."

Ben inquisitively interjects,

"Mia, are you going to be traveling around the country doing signing appearances?"

"Well, Ben, I believe so," she then turns back to Mike to inform him, "I need to talk with you about holding my room for when I return."

"I do believe that will not be a problem, Mia, after all you are, paid up till the end of the year! When do you think you will get started on these signing trips?"

"Well, Mike, I think it could be soon now that the book is out, I'll certainly keep you informed," she turns round to Ben, comforting him, "and yes, you too, Ben."

Ben just sits on the Lobby bench and smiles.

Angel puts down her drink to pick up her phone that is vibrating on the small table, seeing that it's Victor, she answers,

"Hello there, sweet lover man of mine!"

"Hey Hun, what ya been up ta?"

"Not much Victor, sweetheart, I havta' reckon, them malevolent things out there in this here world, is a laying low fir now! And I'm a very much obliged for this break in the action."

"Well, now that was exactly what I was a hopin' for. I'm really so sorry I couldn't come to you last time you asked me to, so I'm hoping you can come to me here in Atlanta for a while, we can do allot of catching up and things! I can call and have a ticket waiting for you at the Baton Rouge Airport tomorra', for any time you'd like. What do you say? Come on, my sweet Angel, come to Atlanta!"

She hesitates for a moment, takes the phone away from her ear, lays it on her chest and sighs, Gabby sees her do this and asks,

"What's a troubling yawl, Sis? Another, job?"

"No, it ain't that, Victor would like me to come to Atlanta and be with him for a while. You be okay, iffin' I go?

"Sure Sis, you go, you sure enough needs it!"

She puts the phone back to her ear,

"Okay, yup, in the mornin', I'll call the DC office and tell em I'm a gonna be taken' a much needed vacation, so have the ticket for me, for an early afternoon flight! And I'll be seein' you in Atlanta, tomorra' later in the afternoon."

"Yes... oh yes! I do love you, so much, I'll even make you your favorite dinner! For our first night."

Mia receives an E-mail from her publisher with a schedule list, of the book signing appearances, they have for her, the first one is in a Barnes & Noble bookstore in Baton Rouge, Louisiana. Then it seems the rest has her traveling to bookstores, making her way back to the Northeast. She thinks,

I'll talk to Mike about this, tonight after dinner.

Just before she goes in for dinner, she stops in the lobby to inform Mike about the E-mail from her publisher, he tells her they will talk about it, after she has her dinner. She agrees and goes into the dining room.

Gabrielle gets a phone call from one of her friends, telling her that the author of the new Vampire book she wants is coming to the Barnes & Noble bookstore in Baton Rouge to do an in store signing this coming Saturday. She excitedly thanks them and goes to the publisher's web site to check on the details. She confirms the date for herself, and marks it on the calendar in red. Her sister Angel had called to tell her the she should be coming home around that time, also. Gabby thinks,

On this coming Saturday I'll go into the bookstore just before closing to avoid the crowd. I do know that they close at nine in the evenin'... Oh wow, it will be so cool to have a signed copy! And I do really want to read it, ever since they announced it was a comin' out soon!

Her thoughts are interrupted by her cellphone ringing, the caller ID shows, Angel,

"Hi Sis how are thinks in Atlanta? I'd reckon, good!"

"Yes, they are. So, yawl behavin'?"

"As usual, sure am!"

"Yeah, I know what your usual is!"

"Oh Sis that new Vampire book I been a wantin is a comin', and the author a gonna be at Barnes & Noble right here in Baton Rouge, for an in store signin' and I'm a goin', this here comin' Saturday night."

"Well, I should be back late Saturday also, maybe I can go with yawl."

"Well, no one is around till later and I want to be there just afer they be closin' up to beat the crowd."

"Yah, don't want ta be standin' in line, huh?"

"Nos' I don't, plus I have some questions for the author, sos' a figgerin' iffin I'm the last customer I can talk with her a bit."

"Okay, then Gabby, I'll sees you when yawl gets yourself home. How you gettin' there?"

"Fixin' to be taken' me, one of them there Ubers."

Mia tells Mike of the signings schedule list, it is quite allot of bookstore locations for her to be at, and she may be away for a little while, Mike assures her,

"Mia, you go do what you must for the success of your first novel, and you're not to be concerned about your home back here, it will certainly be here for you when you return to us."

Mia puts her hand on Mike's, smiles at him saying,

"Thank you Mike, for all your love and concern for me."

"And for Bens' I'd guess."

"Oh, of course, for young Ben, he's the best."

Mike slowly takes his hand from under hers and takes note that her hand felt unpleasantly cold to him, he gives this no more thought and goes about his nightly business

CHAPTER THIRTY-FOUR

MIA ARRIVES AT the Barnes & Noble bookstore in Baton Rouge, Louisiana, on Saturday in mid afternoon, and with the help of an employee they begin to set up the signing table, the signage on all the store windows reads:

~~~~
SHE is here for one day ONLY!
From three to closing,
*Mia Harkness,*
AUTHOR OF HER NEW NOVEL:
'MYSTIC VAMPYRES'
~~~~

The afternoon finished off with only a few sales, Mia sat at the table looking rather sullen. The store employee, Tancy, that was assigned to help her, looks at Mia, smiles and comments,

"Now now there, Ms. Harkness don't yawl be gettin' yourself all sad, the nights are much busier then the days, there'll be plenty more customers comin' in this here evenin' time."

"I sure do hope you are right."

"Coursen' I'm right, Ms. Harkness, I do work here and I knows this here store's traffic. Yous' just wait an see. They'll be a comin' in. Might I be gettin' you something at our in-store Cafe?"

"Yeah, thanks, I could use a cup of tea, please, two spoons of sugar and some milk, would be great!"

"Comin' right at yawl!"

No sooner does Tancy leave for the Cafe, when a line starts forming at the signing table, Mia can hear people in line softly saying: 'yup that's her, she's that new Vampire author, we all been a reading about on the web, this new book of hers is sapposa' to be a real good one, I been a hearin.'

Her book started selling very fast, and she was amazed at all the people wanting a signed copy of it. Tancy comes back with the tea, places it on the table and sits down next to Mia and announces,

"See there now, Ms. Harkness a tolds yawl. Now didn't I, I knows this here store, we's always is, busier at the nighttimes."

"Tancy, please what's with this Ms. Harkness stuff, please do call me Mia."

"Well yah sees, the manager, says we should be a call en' you Ms. Harkness."

"Don't care what your manager says, you can call me, Mia."

"But!"

"No buts, its Mia!"

"Alrighty!, Tancy takes a copy from the pile on the table saying, "And here Mia, sign this here one for me, please."

"I sure will, and it's my treat for the great way you have been taking good care of me."

"Why thanks ya Ms.… I means, Mia!"

"No prob Tancy, but I need a girls' room break."

"We's gots ya covered there, we just puts up this here break sign and yawl can go, I'll stay her by the table, tills ya gets back."

"Thanks."

Mia makes her way to the ladies room, she does her business, and when she goes to the sink to wash up, she looks in the mirror to check her hair, and makeup, she gets a very horrid surprise, because she sees that her eyes for a fleeting moment turn red and she gets the red haze in her vision, which causes her to ruminate,

Oh dear Lord, please please, not here, not now.

She closes her eyes hard for a while, praying for it to stop, which, when she opens them, thankfully they are back to normal.

Back now, at the signing table the crowd is beginning to be thinning out. At the end of it, last one in line, stands Angel's Sister Gabrielle.

Mia leans over to Tancy and says,

"It's slowing down."

"Yup sure is, well the store do close at nine. And it's almost at there now."

"Good, because I am getting a little tired. Have an early flight in the morning, really I will need some sleep."

Tancy sees that Gabrielle is the last in the line, so she takes all but one copy off the table to put them in their place on the store book shelf and says good night. Gratitude and appreciation are exchanged.

Gabrielle stands nervously at the table, slowly puts her copy down, Mia opens it and signs it. Gabby timidly says,

"It's a real pleasure to be meet en' yawl, I've been a wait en all day for this, iffin you don't minds I love to be a asken' yah, about your write ins."

"Sure not a prob, but the store is closing, maybe we could talk if you'd like to walk with me to my Hotel just down the block."

"I'd likes that, and sure would appreciate it, thanks yah."

"Okay then lets go."

They leave the store together and turn in the direction of Mia's Hotel, as they are slowly walking and talking, Mia again gets the red haze in her vision. They begin to pass an alleyway. Mia's Blood Passion, hunger is growing, she gets an idea on how to lore Gabby down the alley. She suddenly stops at the beginning of this alley and takes Gabby by the arm and asks,

"Did you hear that?"

"Hear what?"

"Sounded to me like a muffled call for help from down this alleyway."

"So, whats' should we's do bout it, calls the, Police?"

"No, by the time they get here someone could be hurt real bad, we should go in and see if we can be of any help."

Side by side, they slowly walk in this very dark alley. Mia takes out her cellphone to use as a flashlight, but feloniously claims the battery is too low to do it. Gabby reaches into her jacket pocket to get hers out, but drops it, as she takes it out, and it is so very dark, too dark to see where it fell. In the dark they slowly walk very close together, Mia holds onto Gabby's arm, all they can hear now is, the sound of their shoes on the pavement.

Mia's vision becomes a very opaque red haze, and she now has no trouble seeing in the dark, but she doesn't let on to Gabby, that she can see like it is daytime. Gabby walks slowly and cautiously, depending more and more on Mia for support. This alleyway has become a pitch black abyss, so black, that one cannot see a hand in front of their own face. Suddenly something makes a crashing noise, Gabby startled by this, turns to Mia and hugs her, in fear of the unknown. In doing so she turns her face away from Mia. Mia takes this opportunity of an open access to her neck, so with her fangs now fully extended bites down hard, Gabby goes limp in Mia's arms.

Fortuitously for Gabby the crashing sound is heard again, so before Mia can do a full Blood Passion feeding, she drops her victim to the ground, leaving her there to bleed to death. Mia runs out of the alleyway while converting back to her normal look, not realizing she has kicked Gabby's very distinctive cellphone onto the sidewalk at the beginning of the alleyway.

Mia doesn't stop until she is almost at her Hotel. Taking in a moment to catch her breath, and compose herself before going inside the lobby. She also takes notice that the small amount of her victim's Blood that would always get into her mouth, tasted somewhat different this time, than any other she has ever tasted on her tongue before, distinctly sweeter.

CHAPTER THIRTY-FIVE

A NGEL S ITS A T the kitchen table, with her little dog Bandit, in her lap, repeatedly drumming her right hand nails on the table, and watching the clock, she deliberates,

It's almost ten, I reckoned Gabby would be home by now, she didn't say she'd be going anywhere after the bookstore. So where on this here earth could she be? She would usually call me, iffin' she's running late, or needs a ride.

She anxiously waits another fifteen minutes, she then decides to go look for her sister Gabrielle. Starting with the Barnes & Noble Bookstore.

On the street where the Bookstore is, she pulls over to park her bike, walks to the front door only to find that the place is dark, and locked up tight. She notices the store hours sign reads that they close at nine. She starts to slowly walk back to her bike, keeping a watchful eye out for anything telling, and sure enough, she kicks something with her foot, it traverses along the sidewalk about six feet then stops, then just spins in place. Picking it up, she realizes that there's a very good chance this could be her sister's phone, because of its personalized case with a big glittery G on the back of it, and yes, after a complete examination she concludes that most definitely, it's Gabby's phone. She looks around and listens. Looking now, down the darkened alleyway, she quickly walks back to her bike to get a small but powerful handgun.

Before entering into this ebony abyss of an alleyway, she checks that her weapon is loaded, then turns on the flashlight app on her cellphone, and proceeds slowly and carefully to amble into the alley. About fifteen feet in, she abruptly freezes in place, when she believes she hears a faint, almost like a whispering, someone whimpering in need of help. Very weakly she hears,

"Help, please, someone help me."

She shudders with the realization that it's her sister Gabby's voice. She reacts, by inquiring,

"Hey, is that you Gabby, where are yah?"

"Over here, please hurry, help me."

Angel starts to move her light around frantically looking everywhere. What she sees next, gives her pause, it's a small trail of blood shining in the light from her flashlight, originating, it seems, from some refuse barrels.

She quickly follows it to see someones leg showing from behind a barrel, she grabs hold of this barrel and tosses it aside. She gasps when she shines her light on the face of her sister, Gabrielle.

At first she thinks that, maybe she had been mugged, and would be okay, after some medical attention.

In a very weak, staggering voice Gabby questions,

"An...gel... Angel... is that yawl?"

Angel holsters her gun, squats down and answers,

"Yes, Gabby it is me! What has happened here? Oh, never mind, don't talk, save your strength, you can tell me latea'."

Gabby's head involuntarily moves to expose her neck, where Angel surprisingly sees two small puncture wounds oozing blood, and she knows that these can only be from a bite from a real Vampire,

"Oh dear Lord, Sis, you've been attacked!"

"An...gel... Angel, Angel I'm so sorry, but I think..."

Her words trail off, as suddenly an extremely bright light appears at the end of the alley, then starts to slowly move closer to them. Angel recognizes who, and what is inside this light.

Angel exclaims, as she has knelt down to hold tightly Gabby's now limp body in her arms,

"No, oh no no, Azrael, you can't take her!"

A very supple lucid, but commanding voice comes from the light,

"Angel, Angel Seraph, as you are known here on Earth, her host body has extinguished, I'm here to take her spirit back to whence it came."

She appeals to this 'Angel of Death'; Azreal,

"Just please, you must, give me a moment with her."

She brings Gabby's ear to her lips and whispers asking,

"Who did this to yah?"

Gabby, now with her last dying breath simply, and softly answers,

"The... the author."

Angel holds firmly Gabby's now cold body, turns her face up to the heavens, and swears,

"The author, the author of this book you came here to buy, I will hunt her down, and I... I will kill her for this!"

As the bright light starts to diminish and move away, she hears Azrael's commanding thunderous voice, as Gabrielle's body and clothing disintegrates into ash.

"Thou Shall Not Kill!"

The alley suddenly goes dim, she picks up her phone reactivates the flashlight app, reaches into the ashes to retrieve the book, shakes off the ashes, turns the book over, shines the light on the back cover photo, to discover, with disturbing recognition of this author's picture, she commandingly, avows,

"You? It's you, I know you! I know who yah are, and I well find yah and I will ki... I swear I will make you pay for this!"

At this point she is overcome with emotion, sobbing,

"My, my poor beautiful sister, Gabby!"

She leans forward to grasp some of the ashes in her hand, stands up, just as a strong, sudden gust of wind, seemingly coming from nowhere, through the alley to take the ashes away. They rise up in a swirling motion, lingering for a moment, then after glistening into a cloud of colors, they begin to dissolve and disperse, so do the ashes in her tightly clenched fist. She wipes the tears from her face an slowly walks to the street.

Ironically, a Baton Rouge Police cruiser pulls over and stops, at the beginning of this alleyway, and one of the officers gets out of the car from the passenger side, approaches Angel to ask,

"Cusen' me ma'am, is everthin' okay here?"

"Yes, officer, thanks yah, no problem."

"I'm sorry ma'am, but I has ta ask, does you have a permit for that gun, you're a wearin'?"

She proudly presents her badge to him, explaining,

"Yes, officer, I do, I'm U.S. Marshal, Special Agent Seraph, Angel Seraph."

With that said, he quickly backs away saying,

"You have yourself a fine night now, Marshal Seraph."

As the police car pulls away, she thinks,

Fine night? Could it get any worse? I just lost my only beloved Sister, to what I believe was a real Vampire.

She solemnly approaches her bike, and places the book in one of the saddlebags, mounts the bike, takes her helmet from the handlebar, adorns herself with it, starts it up, engages into gear, and vigilantly pulls away from the curb, in the direction of her home, with only one, singular thought in her mind,

I WILL, find you Mia Harkness, and so help me, make you PAY, for the demise of my beloved Angelic Sister, Gabrielle!

She then turns the throttle grip up full and is gone, into the night.

CHAPTER THIRTY-SIX

ANGEL SITTING ON the deck, finishes reading the 'Mystic Vampyres' novel, closes it and claims,

"This here book is, certainly pure fiction, if there really was this Vampyre cabal. I'd find it! I'd destroy it! Strange how, this author uses her own first name for the name of her main female character, I reckon she be wanten' her readers to think its a real story about herself. Like some kind a autobiography. But it do have, a ring of truth to it, because this here, author of this Vampyre love story novel, Mia Harkness is an actual Vampire, and wouldn't yah knows it a while back, I shared a dinner table with this killa', at the Riverside Bed & Breakfast up there in the state of New York. Darn it, iffin' only I had known what she was then, I'd have taken her down, and my dear Sister, Gabrielle would be alive today."

One tear, trickles down her cheek, because of her remembrance thoughts of Gabby. She rises from the lounge chair to go inside to replenish her drink. Inside now, she places the book on the kitchen table, opens her laptop computer. In the book on the publishers' page she gets the website, so she can learn this author's signing agenda, to be used for tracking this Mia Harkness.

Unfortunately, it may not coincide with her assignments from the U.S. Marshal's department, but she believes she can work around it somehow. If need be she could take herself a leave of absence. The other thing she now needs to consider is a way for her little pal, her dog, Bandit to be cared for while she's away. Suddenly she recollects, that there is a young girl next door that really likes him, and he seems to like her, so she just might be the best choice for this job, she will ask her to do it and pay her well for it. She simply must find, this author Mia Harkness no matter what it takes, but the words of Azrael;

'Thou Shall Not Kill'

Are still ringing in her ears.

As much as she would like nothing more than to kill Harkness, it would be a deal breaker with the powers that be! And then she'd be forced to return to, as Azrael relates, 'from whence she came.' On an oath she swears,

"Harkness, Mia Harkness, I'm a comin' for yawl, yup, I'm a comin' for yah, real soon!"

Mia in her Hotel room in San Francisco, because she doesn't have it memorized, goes over the signings agenda, for her next few Bookstore signing appointments.

She is totally unaware, that U.S. Marshal, Special Agent, Angel Seraph will be dogging her, throughout her travels.

Her next signing appearance is in Seattle, Washington at the Amazon Bookstore, when she observes the one after that she proclaims,

"Oh, wow! I'm going to Las Vegas, that will be so nif! Almost forgot about that one, kinda wish it was for more than one day, and after that, I remember now, it's on to the Windy City, Chicago. And then, oh let me see…"

Abruptly, there comes knocking at her door, she lays the hard copy list down, and calls out,

"Who is it?"

"It's room service, with your breakfast order, Ms. Harkness!"

She answers the door, the person wheels in her breakfast, she thanks him with a healthy tip, has her breakfast, and then gets on her way to the Bookstore signing appointment. The next few signing appointments, seem to go by rather fast, them being one day engagements, it seems she no sooner gets to a location and then it's on to the next, these appearances, being rather successful, they are really generating major interest in her novel.

All the while, unknown by Mia, Angel is trying to be where the website says she will be, but she just can't seem to catch up to her, getting to her location too late, by an hour, or so or mere minutes. Angel, being enormously determined, to catch up with her, because she's not willing to give up the chase. She knows, sooner or later they will come face to face, and then she will get her reckoning, for Gabby's sake.

Likewise, unknown by Angel, is the fact, that she is also under surveillance by the powers that be, to see that she doesn't break the arrangement she had made with them.

Now scrutinizing Mia's agenda, Angel takes note, on Mia's book signing schedule, that in about two weeks, she will be going to New York City, the date she has before that, is in a small town in the New England state of Connecticut, at some quaint Bookstore, Angel would rather have their showdown in 'The Big Apple', after Harkness does her signing at the Barnes & Noble Bookstore. She will now carefully plan accordingly to be there the day before. It's been a long and sometimes grueling chase, crisscrossing the country, nevertheless by no means on this earth, is Angel ready, willing, or able to give up her pursuit of justice, for her Angelic Sister, Gaberielle Seraph.

Mia sits in her Hotel room in Philadelphia sipping a glass of wine, making a check of her E-mail, because the publisher has sent her a text about a not so last minute update to her agenda, that they have already posted to the website, they have received a request for her to do a signing at a small Bookstore in Bank Square at the locality where the story in the novel is supposedly to have taken place; the seaside town of her birth.

She is kindly instructed to go there, before going to New York City. She closes her laptop and with a pout on her face, which slowly turns into a wry smile, she says,

"The return to Mystic! Now, that sounds real bit-chin! It would be so interesting, radicly interesting, like so fetch, for real. Oh, Yeah, Rachael Valli, returns to the town of Mystic, the place of her childhood, as, Mia Harkness, the Author of 'Mystic Vampyres'. Well, okay, just as long as I don't run into Lucy, or my Mom. And what's the chances of that, happening? I think I could pull this off! Even if I do run into them, I mean its only for one day and then off to 'The Big Apple', and speaking of running into people from my past. How's about Shane? He just may still be in New York City, but it's a big city. What could be the chances of that, happening? Mostly a mill to one, I'd guess! So I'll do it, let me see now, it's on Wednesday of this week, real glad it ain't on a Saturday! All right now, Rach… I mean Mia, time to get me some sleep!"

As she lies in bed now, she has a thought,

I really should get me some wheels to drive to NYC, I do think, a motorcycle, like one of them, Honda Shadows, that looks like a Harley Davidson, would be the best think for getting around a city like New York. Yeah, in red, be radicly fetch!

And with that last thought, closing her eyes, she falls off to sleep.

CHAPTER THIRTY-SEVEN

MIA SITS IN her room at the Whaler's Inn, on East Main Street in Mystic, Connecticut, on Tuesday early afternoon of the week she is to do this signing, at the Bank Square Bookshop and then make a move to NYC, for the one on Saturday at the Barnes & Noble Bookstore, while having her light breakfast, she makes a call to the Mystic Motors Dealership, the place that her Grandmother, Carmella Valli had bought her an awesome Motor Scooter when she was younger for her sixteenth birthday. She will inquire about buying a used motorcycle from them.

The dealership receptionist answers her call,

"Hello, Mystic Motors, Good day. How may I direct your call?"

"Well, I'd like to speak with your Sales Persons or person in pre-owned vehicles, please."

"Sure. Who may I say is calling?"

"Yes, um, Mia Harkness.

She waits on hold for about two minutes.

"Hello, Ms. Harkness, I have Frank for you, I'll transfer your call to his office."

She waits on a short hold.

"Hello! Ms. Harkness?"

"Yes. Is this Frank?"

"Yup, I'm Frank, Frank Douglas, at your service! So what can we do for you here at Mystic Motors? But first, Ms. I simply must ask, are you the Mia Harkness, the author of that new novel 'Mystic Vampyres'?"

"Why yes I am!"

"You're here in town for a book signing at our Bank Square bookshop? It's all my daughter has talked about for days, she is so excited to meet you and get your book. You're going to be there this Wednesday, right?

"Yes, I am, Sir."

"So what is it we can do for you, Ms. Harkness?"

"Please, it's Mia, please call me Mia. Well, Frank you see, I need transportation to NYC on Thursday, so I was really hoping you have what I'm looking to buy."

"We certainly will try, Ms. Hark… I mean Mia! So just what is it you are looking for?"

"Okay, this is a long shot I know, but I'm looking for a used; in good shape, Honda Shadow Motorcycle, hopefully in Red, and I will need it by Thursday morning. Is that doable?"

"Okay, let me check what has come in recently, give me a moment, please."

"Yes, of course."

He puts the phone down and rises to go check on their newest inventory, stops suddenly picks it back up and says,

"Wait till my daughter hears, that I spoke with you, she just won't believe it!"

Another short hold.

"Well, Ms. Hark… sorry, Mia, you're in luck we just acquired one in red two days ago, it's been cleaned and getting some light servicing and I believe I can give you a good price on it, too!"

"Super! I'll be in tomorrow. Shall we say around, ten in the morning?"

"Yes, by all means, see you then!"

"Okay now, ciao, till tomorrow!"

Mia, spends the rest of this overcast day leisurely walking around Main Street silently reminiscing about the time she lived and grew up there as herself, first as Rachael Declerico and then as Rachael

Valli, for a while, now in her guise as the author Mia Harkness, in her now died, brunette to blond hair and crystal blue eyes instead of her natural hazel, like her real father Michael Valli had. As she casually strolls the sidewalk, she thinks,

So the people here in Mystic, know about me, and my new novel, it must have been in their local newspaper, I just hope Lucy's not one of those people wanting a signed copy. She just might recognize my voice. So I just won't talk much and I'll keep my head lowered doing signings. Oh yeah, that should work fine.

Mia walks into the lobby of the Mystic Motors, asks for Frank. She is asked to have a seat, and he should be out in a minute. Frank comes into the lobby and he is directed to where Mia is sitting waiting for him, after their mutual introduction, he escorts her to where the bike is, on seeing it she excitedly says,

"Looks awesome, its perfect, I'll take it!"

He answers her,

"I thought you might, so I've drawn up the paperwork already."

"Great! Where do I sign?"

"Please come into my office and we can get it all done."

With the deal done, he tells her,

"Okay, I'll take care of getting it registered, insured and have the plate put on it, so you can take it away tomorrow. That sound alright to you, Ms.... Mia?"

Sounds perfect, see you tomorrow!"

Mia checks the time, her book signing is about to start in an hour, so she walks to the bookshop, goes inside and they have an associate set up the signing table. As usual, it starts off slow, and then picks up as the day wears on. She keeps a vigilance for Lucy, chances are she may be interested in reading the type of novel, Mia has written, and sure enough, she walks in, locates where the signing table is and gets in line. When Lucy gets to the place in line in front of the table, she picks up a copy and places it down in front of Mia, without lifting her head, Mia asks, in a somewhat disguised voice,

"What's your name?"

"It's Lucy, but I think you already knew that."

"Excuse me miss, have we met somewhere before? At another one of my signings. Perhaps?"

"No, not at a signing, it's me… Rachael! It is me, it's me, your old friend Lucy, Lucy Howard!"

"I'm so sorry miss, but I do believe you have me mixed up with someone else, please let the next person in line through, to get a copy."

"But…."

The attendee comes out from behind Mia's chair, takes Lucy gently by her arm, then politely instructs her to take her copy to the register, to pay for it, because she's holding up the line. Lucy tries to resist, claiming,

"But… wait… but I know her, we…."

She is cut off, as the attendee says,

"Ms. Please, you are causing a scene, don't make us have to call the police!"

Lucy pulls her arm away, and goes to the register, mumbling under her breath something about that, this author is really her old childhood friend, Rachael Valli.

The attendee tries to console her by saying,

"Yes Ms., we would all like to know this new author."

"But, I'm trying to tell you…."

"Please Ms., just step outside, and calm yourself down."

Outside now, Lucy takes a deep breath, and dials Rachael's Mother Mina, on her cellphone, no sooner does Mina answer Lucy frantically says,

"Mrs D, it's her, I know it's her!"

"Lucy? You know who, is her, who?"

Lucy explains, and tells Mia that she needs to get down here to the Bookshop right away and see for herself.

"Lucy my dear, I'm at an important game of Mathew's, I just can't leave now, and it's going into a late finish."

"Oh Mrs. D, but I tell yeah it's her. I just know it is!"

"Lucy please stop this, I need to go, we can talk tomorrow about it! Okay?"

"Okay, Mrs. D, but...."

Mina ends the call, before Lucy can finish what she was starting to say. Lucy puts her phone in her back pocket and slowly starts to walk away from the shop, she turns the book over to view the author picture and thinks,

It's you, Rachael, I just know it's you, you are alive! I just feel it, you are, alive!

She stops, looks back at the shop, then continues slowly walking away as her eyes well up and a tear rolls down her cheek.

In the morning, Mia acquires the bike, then is on her way to her business in NYC. Arriving one day before the signing, she registers at the Plaza Hotel and relaxes in her room.

CHAPTER THIRTY-EIGHT

NEW YORK CITY on a Friday morning, is an extremely bustling place to be in, with people rushing around to get to where ever they are going. Mia decides to go out for her breakfast. Just as Mia exits, one elevator, Angel gets on another to be taken to her room. Mia leaves the Plaza Hotel to walk down Fifth Avenue, heading for Columbus Circle, looking for a coffee shop, as luck would have it, she finds one, that is not too busy, she enters and gets into a short line, finally she gets a cup of coffee and a place to sit at a very small table for two, she sips her coffee, with her head down looking at a newspaper someone left behind, suddenly someone is standing at her table and he asks,

"Cuse me, ma'am., but would you mind much iffin' I sit at your table to have my coffee?

She thinks,

'Ma'am... iffin'? Only one man I've ever known in my life to have used these words, is Shane! Could it be him? What are the chances, but there is no way he could recognize me, now with blond hair and blue eyes.

So, she slowly lifts her head from the paper, to surprisingly see who is asking to sit down, and sure enough its him, a little older, a little heavier, but it is him; Shane, Shane Smith, the man, her first real love and lover, that she had to lose back in Mystic, for his protection against her condition. He sits and inquires of her,

"So Ms., you here, in 'The Big Apple' on business?"

"Yeah, you could say that, I'm Mia Harkness, an Author with a new novel doing a signing tomorrow, at the Barnes & Noble bookstore."

"Might I ask, the name of your book?"

She reluctantly answers him,

"It is 'Mystic Vampyres'."

Suddenly, that title triggers an old memory in his mind,

Mystic Vampires?... Well iffin' my memory serves me right, weren't Rachael Valli writin' a manuscript about Vampires back in Mystic, Connecticut some time ago. But this can't be her, it don't look like her, but she do sound a little like her, but that was so long ago I can't be sure, sure enough to ask her iffin' she is, and it just wouldn't be polite to do so.

While Shane is deep in his thoughts, Mia takes notice, that his left hand that is holding his coffee cup, has a wedding ring on it. Shane breaks the silence, saying,

"Oh, man, where's my manners," he puts his hand out across the table and continues, "I'm Shane, Shane Smith of MusicSmith, I'm a DeeJay mostly at the NYC Dance Club, it's real nice to have met yawl!"

"Likewise", She answers, and thinks,

But, I know your name, and I know who you are. And I know... what I'm still, feeling for you.

He rises from the chair to leave, saying,

"Well I needs to be going now, so a book signin' at the Barnes & Noble Bookstore tomorra', huh, just might be, I'd come by and get me a signed copy of your book for, my wife Cheryl. Nice to have met you, bye, have a good day!"

She reciprocates, and forlornly thinks, as she watches him leave,

It's nice to have seen you again, Shane. Always wondered what that would be like, and feel like, it wasn't as bad as I thought it would be, I'd hazard a guess, it would have gone quite differently if he had recognized me, as my real self, the girl he once knew, Rachael Valli.

Mia spends the rest of her day doing a little shopping at Macys, for a new outfit for the signing. Ironically, she leaves the store by one exit, as Angel arrives using a different entrance, it being, much too busy, with people in a rush coming and going, they wouldn't have noticed each other anyway.

Angel uses this day, before Mia's sighing to check on the location of the bookstore and the streets and avenues around it right up to and in, Central Park. She will have to kind of stakeout the place to see just how Mia arrives, fortuitously for Angel, there is signage on the front door, and windows, announcing her signing time, to be three pm to closing, also telling of her location in the store. She realizes that she can not confront Mia, while she's inside the store, so she will need to wait until she comes out, luckily there is only one entrance to the store, so the way Mia goes in, is the exit she will be coming out to the street. Also Angel, takes into account that it will be nighttime, and that the cover of darkness just might be an advantage for a Vampire. She will make certain she has her night vision equipment with her. Any advantage Angel will have is that she's a U.S. Marshal, so she can park her bike almost anywhere she wants to, just in case Mia takes any kind of motorized transportation, she can be right on her tail. Her motorcycle being, the best way in New York City to maneuver around, like in any big city. She only hopes Mia has not thought about that.

Lucy pulls up the driveway on the Motor Scooter, that Rachael had given to her for a birthday present a while ago, to the back door of Mina DiClerico's house in Mystic, which respectfully she refers to her as Mrs. D, Mina hears the scooter, and comes out to greet her,
"Lucy my dear, it's nice to see you. However, why have you come?"
Excitedly, Lucy explains, as she dismounts the scooter,
"Well, Mrs. D, I wanted to see and talk to you, and show you the author's picture on the back cover of this book 'Mystic Vampyres' by Mia Harkness, to see want you think, about the incident relating to the, Main Square Bookshop occurrence on Wednesday, I'd say yes, Mrs. D, it's her, its her this Mia Harkness is really your Daughter

Rachael, alive! I've seen some of the manuscript of this book, when she had started writing it, and it's just about the same stor…"

Mia cuts her off,

"Lucy, please stop and come inside, have a seat and calm down, you're all hyper! You need to relax, and yes, I will have a look at this author's photo, please Lucy come in."

Lucy with the book in question enters into the kitchen, and reluctantly has a seat at the table. Mina asks her if she would like something to drink. Lucy requests,

"I'd like a soda, Cola if you have one, please."

Mina puts the soda on the table in front of Lucy, as she takes a seat. Lucy places the book down in front of Mina with the back cover showing and proclaims,

"Mrs. D, please, with all due respect, is this or is this not your Daughter, Rachael?" Lucy starts tapping her finger on the picture, "I'll admit there are a few minor differences, but look, just look, I tell ya it was her, I just know it was, I heard her voice, it was Rachael's voice, oh, Mrs. D, if only you could have been there!"

"Lucy, you know why I wasn't there," Mina looks at the Photo and claims,

"Wait… you say, minor differences? This young woman author has blonde hair, my Rachael, had brunette, and this woman's eyes are blue, Rachael had Hazel.

"Yes, that's true Mrs. D, so she most likely dyed her hair, and she's wearing eye color changing contacts. Also, what about her name? Huh?"

"Lucy what about, her name?"

"Okay, so Mrs. D, your first name is Mina, with your maiden name Harper, so we have Mina Harper, and she uses Mia Harkness. Pretty close wouldn't you say?"

"Lucy, I do think you'd make a pretty good detective, but I'm sorry, I believe that your elaborating on some coincidences here just a bit too far for your own good, because you miss her so much and want her to be alive, and I sympathize with you, I'd like nothing more than to have my Rachael back with us."

"But, Mrs. D, please, I know it was her, for me it was a very strong feeling. I mean when we were together, and that was a lot, she'd inhale, and I'd exhale, I loved her like the sister, I never had."

At this point Lucy begins to cry. Through her tears she says,

"I… I, just mi… miss her so much!"

Mina reaches over to the counter behind her to get Lucy a tissue, and handing it to her attempts to comfort her, consolingly saying,

"Here, Lucy, my dear sweet Lucy, we all do!"

Lucy composes herself and slowly gets up to leave,

They hug with a mutual kiss on their cheeks, and Lucy goes outside. Mina follows her out, as Lucy mounts the scooter and starts it up, but before she puts on her helmet, Mina requests,

"Lucy, please be careful driving the scooter!"

Lucy musters a smile, and replies,

"Always, Mrs. DiClerico, always!"

Mina waves to Lucy, as she drives out the driveway onto the street, thinking,

That poor sweet young girl, claiming that an author of a Vampire novel, being my deceased daughter, is a little too much for me to imagine. Dear Lord, I've had just about enough, involvement with Vampires in my life. Too much more than enough, actually!

From inside the house, she hears her son, call to her,

"Mom!"

As she walks in, through the door, she answers him,

"Coming, Mathew!"

CHAPTER THIRTY-NINE

NEW YORK CITY Barnes & Noble Bookstore, at two o'clock in he afternoon, is not a very busy place, even though the sidewalks are packed with people dashing from place to place.

Angel arrives outside the Bookstore roughly at two forty-five, parks her bike about a block away. Expecting for Harkness to appear sometime around three, she stands concealed across the street, in a doorway shadow, armed with only her silver blade, she knows that brandishing a firearm in a large city can cause chaos.

After about ten minutes a person riding a red motorcycle pulls into the internal parking lot, just down the street from the store, in which Angel has a clear line of sight to, not sure who it might be, she waits to see who just might show up soon now, and sure enough, Harkness comes walking down the street with a red helmet under her arm and into the store.

Angel thinks,

So that most likely was her on that red bike, she's no fool she acquired a motorcycle, she's smarter than I thought she'd be. So it's lookin' like it just might be a motorcycle chase through the streets of New York City, and I'd havta' reckon' she has most likely, checked out the way the streets are laid out for getting here.

She has a reminding thought for herself, rule number one, Angel: *Never, ever underestimate your opponent. From what I remember, when we shared a dinner table together, at the Riverside Bed and Breakfast, up there in Sleepy Hollow, New York, she is a smart young woman. I mean after all, she is a writer, and also some kind of weird Vampire, with I'd havta' say, a thinking ahead frame of mind. I now have to out think her, if I'm going to accomplish my mission, but for now, it's a waiting game.*

Angel continues to think and plot, as she walks to her bike to disarm and remove her outer biker leather apparel, to reveal her street clothing, Angel now walking back to the bookstore, continues with her thinking,

So now that I don't look so menacing, I shall go into this Bookstore, and have a look at her, and get some coffee and something to eat in their café. I don't believe she knows that I'm on her trail, and she shouldn't be a going anywhere, too soon, with all her book signin' to do.

As she's making her way to where the book signing area is, she notices a young woman in a baseball cap and sunglasses, looking rather suspicious, kind of hiding behind a bookshelf petition, in the line of sight of the signing table. Angel doesn't recognize, of what she can see of her, so pays her no mind, and goes off to the café to get herself some coffee and a little something to eat.

As Angel enjoys her little snack, she resumes her thoughts,

Well, where she most likely has no idea that I'm after her for the death of my sister, Gabrielle, back there in Baton Rouge, I most certainly do have the upper hand, givin' me the element of surprise, I would havta' say.

Around five o'clock Mia's book signing started to get busy, the line had a good amount of people desiring a signed copy of her novel. The signing table closed at six for a dinner break of about thirty minutes. Angel outside now, dressed in her riding leathers, checks the time, she realizes that it won't be long now, since the store closes at nine, it's almost eight.

At about eight thirty, Shane shows up to get a copy for his wife, he takes a place in line. The young woman with the hat and sunglasses on, that is keeping out of sight, off in the distance, maintaining a vigilant watch on what is going on, notices him, believing she recognizes this man, as Shane Smith the DeeJay, from the Cliff House, house warming party back in Mystic. She wonders if he knows who this author Mia Harkness really is. Perceiving that he will most likely be the last one to get a copy, she will wait to make her appearance after he has acquired his. Then she will use an element of surprise, to catch this author off guard, so as to reveal her true identity.

Shane steps up to the table puts his copy down in front of Mia. She looks up and says,

"So you really do want a signed copy of my book."

"Yup, well, it's for my Wife, she kinda' likes these sorta' stories. And her birthday is next week, so…"

"So what's her name?"

"Her name is Cheryl."

She signs it, and hands it back to him saying,

"Here you are, Sir, I really hope that she likes it!"

"Well, I reckon the store is closing now, might I escort you to your transportation. New York at night, can be a rough town for a woman alone."

"That would be very gallant of you. My transportation is parked just down the street in the garage, and yes, I'd like that very much. Thank you!"

"It'd be my pleasure, ma'am."

"Okay then, Sir, I'll wait at the door for you while you pay for your book."

Just as Shane is starting to leave the table, this young woman with the hat and sunglasses on, reveals herself from behind the partition at the back of the signing table. Throwing off her hat and glasses she proclaims excitedly,

"Racheal, Rachael Valli, it's me, Lucy, I know it's really you Rachael!"

Mia, rather startled quickly stands up, looking at her with a wry smile on her face, at the same time Shane stops, turns round and claims,

"Racheal? I thought it was you, " as he points to Lucy he continues, "And you, you're her friend Lucy from Mystic. Just what's goin' on here?"

Mia declares,

"Sir... I mean Shane, please, I'm sorry, I'll explain as you walk me to the parking garage."

"Okay, see, yeah at the exit door."

Lucy steps closer to Mia, now revealed as her true self, hugging her, she elatedly proclaims,

"I knew it... just knew it, you're, you are alive, alive!"

"Lucy, please, Lucy you're making a scene... again!"

Lucy holds on to her tighter, as Mia requests,

"Lucy, just let me go, we can talk soon and I'll explain."

With that, Lucy releases her, and Mia starts for the exit door to wait for Shane.

All the while, U.S. Marshal, Angel Seraph is outside, across the street, just patiently waiting for Harkness to come out.

CHAPTER FORTY

SHANE MAKES HIS purchase of the book, at the register, then goes to the door to see this author Mia Harkness to the parking garage, which he now knows is really his ex-lover, Rachael Valli, formerly of Mystic. As Mia is making her way for the door to meet with Shane, she is abruptly stopped again, by a persistent Lucy, who quickly stands in front of her, barring her way,

"Rachael, you are going to tell me what happened to you back in Mystic, and why!"

"Yes, Lucy, but not here, and not now! Please, get out of my way, I'll tell you later."

She, now feeling a strange urgency, gives Lucy a gentle push to the side, and quickly walks to the door where Shane is waiting. They exit the store together, and begin to walk down the street toward the parking garage. Angel slowly begins to follow them, wondering who the man is with her, she thinks,

Dear lord, she has found herself another victim, so I'll finally be gettin' her, an be a savin' a life, to boot.

Unfortunately for Angel, they are walking in the direction away from where her bike is parked on the street, she does not realize this right away, it dawns on her as she looks back, to see her bike down the street.

Mia, and Shane are strolling along leisurely, engaging in some small talk, Angel quickens her pace to close the distance between them, as she comes within earshot calling out to Shane,

"Cuse me, Sir, you don't really want ta be a goin' with this woman."

Shane stops short, tells Mia to keep walking, he turns round with his hand poised on his concealed handgun that he normally wears and responds,

"So tell me, ma'am, just why would I'd, not want to be goin', with this woman?"

"Please, Sir, take your hand off what, I reckon, is a concealed firearm."

While saying this, she shows her badge, taps her holstered gun on her hip, identifying herself,

"I am United States, Marshal, Special Agent, Angel Seraph, this woman bein' a real, and genuine Vampire is wanted for murder, the murder of my Sister, and I'd havta' think others also!"

The light of the street lamp post illuminates her badge enough for Shane to see that she is for real, so he takes his hand away from his firearm, and displays to her, that his hand is empty.

She reiterates,

"Now, please get away from her, and just be a leavin' her to me!"

Meantime, Mia, keeps walking toward the garage, hearing a little of what is being said, but not very sure what was ensuing, but Shane did tell her to keep going. She quickens her pace almost to a run, and then ducks into the parking garage, disappearing out of sight, to be able to get her bike. She moves quickly to the booth, handing the attendant two twenties, and declares,

"Here, this auta' cover it!"

Then snatches up her keys from the board, and runs to where she remembers, the place the attendant told her to park her bike when she arrived.

Out on the sidewalk, Shane is doing his level best, to hold up the U.S. Marshal in order to give Rachael time to get away. Every time Angel tried to advance toward the garage he would block her way, and try to keep her talking. She finally, authoritatively demands of him, as she brandishes her handcuffs,

"Now look here Sir, yawl are obstructing justice, don't make me arrest yah for it."

At that moment a red motorcycle comes screaming out from the garage, turns down the street away from where Shane and Angel are contesting. She gives up trying to get around him, and turns away from him quickly to go for her bike, to go after Mia, and chase her down, through the streets of 'The Big Apple' at night. When she reaches her bike its only a matter of seconds before she's underway in pursuit, of this murdering Vampire. Angel thinks,

She will not get away from me this time, I will get her for yah, Gabrielle, she is gonna' pay.

Angel catches sight of her, headed toward Central Park, they both weave in and out of traffic, until Rachael enters into the Park, just narrowly avoiding someone walking out, the chase is not long, as Rachael goes off the park utility road onto a walking path almost hitting a tree, but as she avoids that one she hits another, and goes down. The bike now lying on her leg, she's not able to get up to run away. She desperately struggles to get free.

Angel, which was in close pursuit, stops her bike dismounts, takes her Shotgun from the front fork, pumps it once making certain it's loaded, then slowly walks over, to where her Sister's murderer is lying trapped on the ground with the bike on her leg. Rachael's strugglings to get free, brings out her Vampire elements, so giving her the extra strength that is needed to lift the bike off of her leg, in doing so she shakily scrambles to her feet. Angel postured close with her Shotgun, hip aimed at the heart of this now, clearly looking Vampire, says,

"Finally, I've caught up with yah, and you're a real one, the real thing, a Vampire, that murdered my poor innocent, unsuspecting Sister Gabrielle, back there in Baton Rouge outside the Barnes & Noble Bookstore, and, now, you're a gonna' pay for it."

Rachael, now on her feet, still a little shaky, catches her breath, giving Angel a good look with her now red Vampire eyes, realizing that she knows this woman, recognizing her now, from the time they had dinner together one night long ago, at the Riverside Bed and Breakfast, up in Sleepy Hollow, New York. Angel raises the gun to her shoulder, takes aim, as Rachael holds up her hands to defend herself, and plead her case,

"Wait, please, Marshal I didn't kno... im so so sorr... please, it wasn't anything personal... please try to understand, I just..."

Before Rachael can finish, she begins to turn slightly away, attempting to run, Angel sees this, and fires! Hitting her in the shoulder, sending her back off her feet, to slam hard up against a tree, and blacking out.

Angel slowly lowers her weapon, walks to where Rachael is in a seated position on the ground, up against the tree, bleeding profusely, seemingly unconscious. She makes a slight attempt to wake her to see if she is still alive, in getting no responds, she feels she has done enough, and decides to leave her there, so when the sun comes up it should finish her off. Figuring,

Well, it will be the sun that will kill her, for me, and for Gabby.

Angel, with her weapon now by her side gets to her bike mounts it, breathes a large sigh of relief, and has what she hopes is the final thoughts on this event,

Well, ma' dear sweet Sister, it is done, we both should rest easy a' now, Gods' created elements, will finish her off, and on that note, I'm finished myself, and could very much be needin' some good sleep.

She places the Shotgun securely back to the fork, puts on her helmet, starts the bike and makes her way to the Plaza Hotel.

EPILOGUE

RACHAEL'S EYE LIDS start to vacillate as she begins to wake, she is brought to full consciousness as she begins to feel the excruciating discomfort in her shoulder, that suddenly makes its self known to her, she moves her hand to it only to feel more pain when she touches it, takes her hand and looks at it only to find that her hand is now covered in her blood, she holds back from crying out in pain, she also notices that the sun is coming up and in her weakened condition it could be deadly to her.

At first she believes that, she has passed out again from the pain, for what she is seeing can only be a dream, or a nightmare. For standing over her is a shadowy shape that appears to have wings, this mysterious image kneels down on one knee in front of her, lays their hand on her injured shoulder and suddenly, she is healed, and her pain is gone. It then whispers in her ear,

"Please, make not a sound, do not speak, I've been sent to help you, Angel Seraph should not have tried to kill you, she has broken the sacred agreement, just in the intent to execute a living being, we know what was in her mind, we do sympathize with her feelings. That is why our kind has no emotions, like your kind does, to be motivated by emotions is erroneous for us to do, we are only motivated by logic, we only do what we know is best. So I, Angel Cherub have been sent to undo what she has done, and because you are much too weak to do it yourself, I will transport you to a safe place for you to hide in the shadows for you to recover enough, for you to go your way."

Angel is awakened by a knocking at her room door, she leans up slowly on her elbows and curiously inquires,
"Who is it?"
A somewhat muffled voice comes from outside the door,
"Room service!"
"I didn't order any room service for this mornin'. Go away!"
More knocking,
"Please, Ms. it could mean my job if, I don't deliver your order."
She unwillingly gets out of bed, adorns herself with her robe saying,
"All right all right, I'm a comin'!"
At the door now, she agitatedly throws it open, and she hears.
"SURPRISE!"
She blinks and says,
"Victor, Victor what are ya…?"
He gently backs her up inside the room, while closing the door with his foot, then gives her a quick kiss and says,
"Don't yah rememba', two days ago you text me to tell me yah would be here today, so I flew up here to see yah."
"It musta' slipped my mind, that's real nice of yah, and I do so love, to be seeing yah, but I need to go to the New York U.S. Marshal's office this here mornin'. To check in!"
"That's fine, yah do that, and then I'll take yah for lunch at the 'Tavern on the Green' Restaurant, yah always sayen' you want to go there next time you be here in New York City, and whata' ya' know, here we are, in 'The Big Apple' together, I'll go get us a reservation for lunch, so you go to the office and text me when yah done, I'll send a car round to get you to bring you to the Restaurant, where I'll be a waitin' on yah."

As Rachael now has the strength to get to her room at the Plaza Hotel, it just so happens that she will be passing by the 'Tavern on the Green' Restaurant. As she does, she glances in the window and happens to notice Angel is sitting, holding hands across the table with a man, she activates her enhanced Vampiric hearing just in time to catch the end of their conversation, she hears Angel saying,

"Oh, my, now, Mister Victor Vincent, yah do be a sayin' the sweetest thins' to me!"

"Angel, my sweet Angel, my Darlin', sayin', I love you just comes, natural to me, cause I do!"

Rachael backs away from the window, to continue on to her room at the Plaza Hotel, thinking,

So this, Mister Victor Vincent is her weakness, good to know.

The End?

J. M. VALENTE's
BLOOD PASSION

Novels Series;
Book I,
Book II,
&
Book III

Contact info;
E-Mail
jimvalente@comcast.net

Two Chapter preview of:

BLOOD PASSION
BOOK V
RACHAELS' REVENGE

ONE

MIA SLOWLY MAKES her way back to the New York City, Plaza Hotel elevator area, still feeling a little weak, she leans herself up against the wall, presses the up button and impatiently waits for the elevator to arrive, the lift door finally slides open, she enters this empty elevator, somewhat unsteady on her feet, the lift operator notices, so displaying concern inquires,

"Pardon me Ms., are you alright?"

"Yes, I'm just fine, please, I just need to get to my room."

The operator requests,

"Floor, please?"

She replies, the door closes, the elevator begins to

swiftly rise, stopping on her floor, she exits saying,

"Thanks!"

As she, slow but sure, makes her way to her room she reflects,

This U.S. Marshal Seraph clearly wanted me dead for the taking of her Sister's life, and she clearly could have killed me, but something stopped her. And she only knows me as the, blond, blue eyed, author Mia Harkness, now would be the perfect time to go back to my real name, and identity, so glad I kept all my original identification stuff, I can now, go back to being the, brunette, hazel eyed, Rachael Valli of the town of Mystic.

She gets into her room puts her phone on the bedside table, lollops into the bed, to get some more much needed rest, closing her eyes she quickly falls off to sleep. She hears someone calling to her, using her real name,

"Rachael, Rachael Valli."

She sluggishly leans up on her elbows, to observe an undulating shadowy figure, with some things protruding out from behind it, standing at the foot of her bed, she inquires softly uttering,

"Who are…?"

A voice from this shadow interrupts her, it sounds somewhat familiar, but still quite strange,

"Rachael, the motorcycle you were driving is still in the park, it's under the Laguardia walkway bridge, I moved it there for you, I do believe it is still in working order."

Sleepily she answers,

"Huh, oh, yah, my Bike, I will be needing it, I suppose I should say, thanks. But, wait, who… who are you?"

"I was sent to you in the Park, to right a wrong that had been done, what she did, or was trying to do to you, is forbidden. I wasn't in time to stop her, but I was in time to save you."

"Like I said, I should thank you, but…"

"I know what you are going to say; that I saved a life that is cursed, maybe you'd be better off if I had just let you die."

"Exactly!"

"All life is precious, no matter what kind it is, it is a Gift. It is the 'Greatest' Gift!"

"Well, my Gift, as you put it, is one of horror, and dread. You do know what I am? You must!"

"Yes, we do know what you are, and how you came to be, and what you are compelled to do to survive, and it was put upon you unintentionally, you are the love child of a Vampire, your Father, and a human, your Mother, they had no idea what they would be creating, and this can not be undone, now I'm sorry but you will, and must live the life you were born to."

"You are… you're… sorry?"

"Yes, because there is no way to change what you are, it is not within, the powers that be, to alter you, from what you were born to be, again I'm sorry, there is nothing that can be done about it."

"Oh, well then, I guess I should thank you for saving my life."

"You are welcome, just live it the best that you can, is all I can ask in the return of your, gratefulness to us."

"Yes, yeah, okay. Us?"

Suddenly her cellphone on the bedside table rings, and wakes her. She opens her eyes, slowly sits up, and answers it,

"Hello?"

"Yes, hello Ms. Harkness?"

"Yes, who's cal…?"

"It is, Ms. Able from your publisher, calling to remind you of your last book signing appearance in Boston this coming weekend. So, how did the New York one go?"

"Just great, and thanks for calling, not to worry, I'll be there."

"Good, safe journey!"

"Yes, thanks, goodbye."

She hangs up, looks at the cellphone to get what day it is, she thinks,

I've some time before I need to leave New York City for Boston, so I'll go get my Bike, take myself a ride along the waterfront tonight, I surely could use a Blood Passion feeding. This one in Boston is the last of my signing tour, so then I'll get back to being who I really am, then find out about who this Mr. Victor Vincent is. Oh, Rachael, you can be so bad, bad bad bad. But, I need, what I need!

In the early evening she finds her red Honda Shadow Motorcycle lying under the bridge, just where she was told it would be. She takes a look around, sees that no one is about at the moment, so she brings out her Vampire powers, that will give her the strength she needs to lift it up, it looks okay, so she mounts it, starts it up, takes the red, full face tinted Helmet from the handlebars and puts it on. Slowly now she drives it out to the street. It's a little to early to cruise the harbor, so she'll take a spin around the City. As she's casually cruising, the U.S. Marshal, Angel Seraph, that would have liked to destroy her, but only assaulted her with deadly force, then left her there in Central Park unconscious, for when the sun came up it would finish her off, walking with her Man, this Mr. Victor Vincent, together on the sidewalk of the street, she is riding on, observing them she speeds up and rides passed them, as no more than a red blur. Angel catches sight of this Bike and Rider, thinking,

No… could ant' be? I'd reckoned the sun musta' destroyed her, no one could have showed up to help her. I havta' figga' there are plenty a' red Motorcycles in this here big City. So that ain't her.

Victor, takes note of Angel's deep in thought silence, so asks,

"Angel, why yuh so quiet? Somethin' on your mind?"

"No my love, ain't nothin' on my mind, just enjoyin' my walk with you here in 'The Big Apple'!"

"So my love, any of them there secret assignments comin' for yah any time soon?"

"No my sweet, they didna' say there was any, when I met with them this here mornin'. I'll just call em' tomorrow."

"Good, that's a meanin' we have tonight to…"

Before he can finish, she cuts him off,

"Oh, me oh my… my dear Mr. Victor Vincent, yah can be a mite devilish at times!"

"Yup, I can, yawl complainin'?"

"Not at all, Sir! Not one bit!"

"Good! Let's get us a drink in the Plaza Hotel Lounge."

"Yup, I'm a surely like in', that idea!"

TWO

MIA SLOWLY CRUISES along the New York City Waterfront District, it's not quite nightfall, yet, but the sun is getting low in the sky, no need for her night vision right now. So she will scope out the lay of this borough, checking out just where the deviants hang out. Then she will return when it is darker to find and acquire herself a reluctant Blood donor for her much needed Blood Passion, hence replenishing her strength back to what it was before her encounter, in Central Park with the U.S. Marshal, Special Agent, Angel Seraph. She will need to be at her full strength capacity before heading to Boston for her last appearance as Mia Harkness. Then, it will be adios' Mia Harkness, welcome back Rachael Valli.

She must, and she will find a way to bring Rachael Valli back into the world, so she contemplates,

Just as I had successfully planned, and accomplished a way of faking my own death, and disappearing, back there in Mystic, when I was under the assumption that the authorities were closing in on me. Now I need to, somehow, do the reverse. All that, I'll strategize it out later, after I get my much needed Blood Passion feeding, while I'm making my way up to Boston.

It will be dark enough, very soon now, for her to find a victim for her Blood Passion feeding. So for now, she just cruises around the City, killing time before it's her 'Killing Time'. Then check out and then make her way north, off to Boston, to check in at a place, she will call for a room reservation for one, maybe two nights.

After a lovely room service dinner for herself, and her man, Angel gets a call from the U.S. Marshal's Washington DC Office, she answers,

"Hello? This is Special Agent, Angel Seraph!"

"Yes, we have Director Hughes, he is waiting for you. Please hold."

As she brings the phone away from her ear, Victor asks,

"What is it that you think, they want?"

"A call at this hour, it must be something urgent."

Just as she brings the phone back to her ear she hears,

"Angel, hello, sorry to call so late, but we've something that needs your attention asap! We have received a serious request for your presence in Paris, France.

I have our jet on standby, and as usual, I'll send you the details, before you take off, so you can study it on your flight over there, and of course you can bring your bike. So what do you think?"

"What do I think? Just hold on please."

She lowers the phone giving Victor an inquisitive look and asks of him,

"Hey, my lover man, would ya like to go to France with me? I have an assignment over there, please say yawl will come."

"Well, I will have till next week, to get back to work," and with a slight hesitation he answers her,

"Heck yeah, I'd love to go!"

"Great! Start packing, we leave immediately!"

She puts the phone up to her mouth and says,

"Director, I'll gladly take this hear assignment, just as long as I can take my Victor with me."

"Angel, my dear, no need for you to ask that, of course you can. The plane is waiting at JFK, with all the usual clearances. Have a safe flight."

"Thank you, sir, I'll be checking for your info E-mail at the Airport before we board. Can you tell me now, anything of what it's about?"

"Well, all I can say right now is, that, it has to do with something they are referred to as, the 'Nightstalker'!"

Now being dark enough, Mia heads over to New York's Waterfront to acquire what she seriously needs.

She spots what appears to be a lone deviant standing by a barrel on a small, rather dark pier, with water on both sides of it. She parks her bike close by, and as she slowly walks toward him she brings out her Vampire night vision to see that, yes, he is exactly what she needs. As she walks by without looking at him, he does notice that she is a young woman and inquires of her,

"Hey there, young woman, what yeah doing in this part of the City at this hour? It's not a good or safe place for anyone to be in at night!"

Without turning her head it his direction she brings out her other Vampire attributes and says,

"Yes, I can see that, and I'll be really glad to show you why!"

Now, she turns around to notice, that he has not turned to be facing her, so she swiftly comes up from behind him. Quickly wrapping her left arm around his neck, bending him back and down toward her, holding him fast, she places her right hand on his forehead, pulling his head back, and to the side, to get a clear opening to his neck, so she can quickly sink her fangs into his flesh, and faster than ever before, sucks in all of his blood. As this now used body goes limp in her arms, she moves over to the edge of the pier, where she can just let go to let it fall into the water. With this done, she shifts her clothing and listens to hear anything that could be a threat to her, with her strength now replenished, and feeling very confident she laughs and thinks,

Like anything in this City could ever be a threat to me now at this time, when I now have back my restored full Vampire abilities, that I can bring out when needed.

With these thoughts, she relaxes, so to let her return to her human look of, Mia Harkness. Noticing her image in the moonlit water, she scours at her reflection, then goes to where her bike is parked, to get to the Plaza Hotel, to pack up, check out, and leave New York City for Boston.

After packing, she makes a call to a prominent Hotel in Downtown Boston for a room for two nights.

As she now makes her way out of the City, ironically, her bike and Angel's bike pass each other on the street speeding off in opposite directions. After they pass by one another, Mia has is what she hopes is a final thought concerning Angel,

She may believe, she has destroyed the Vampire, Mia Harkness, but she has as of yet, to meet the Vampire,

Rachael Valli!

www.ingramcontent.com/pod-product-compliance
Lightning Source LLC
LaVergne TN
LVHW011938070526
838202LV00054B/4716